ROBERT WESTALL

HAUNTINGS

OLD MAN ON A HORSE

"It's an old man on a horse." Tobias said it quick as a flash. He only wondered afterwards how he was so sure it was an *old* man on the horse. How he seemed to recognize it. Or did it recognize him?

For he knew from that start that it was magic. It had . . . life inside it. Like the brass Buddha Dad kept in the bedroom at home. Only much, much more magic than the Buddha. A grim, black, battered magic. He squatted back on his heels, wondering if it was evil. He wished he'd never found it.

Other titles in the HAUNTINGS series:

Ghost Abbey by Robert Westall
Don't Go Near the Water by Carolyn Sloan
Voices by Joan Aiken
The Nightmare Man by Tessa Krailing
A Wish at the Baby's Grave by Angela Bull
The Bone Dog by Susan Price
All on a Winter's Day by Lisa Taylor

8

ROBERT WESTALL

HAUNTINGS

OLD MAN ON A HORSE

Hippo Books
Scholastic Publications Limited
London

Scholastic Publications Ltd.,
10 Earlham Street, London WC2H 9RX, UK

Scholastic Inc.,
730 Broadway, New York, NY 10003, USA

Scholastic Tab Publications Ltd.,
123 Newkirk Road, Richmond Hill,
Ontario L4C 3G5, Canada

Ashton Scholastic Pty. Ltd.,
P O Box 579, Gosford, New South Wales,
Australia

Ashton Scholastic Ltd.,
165 Marua Road, Panmure, Auckland 6,
New Zealand

Published simultaneously in hardback by Blackie & Son Ltd, and in paperback by
Scholastic Publications Limited, 1989

Copyright © Robert Westall, 1989

ISBN 0 590 76082 3

Chapter One

Tobias awakened in his bunk in the bus. He rubbed the mist off the big window. It was a lovely morning, the sun hardly up. Across the yard the chimney was smoking; Mum getting breakfast.

The bottom bunk was still full of Greta. A tiny coiled-up hump and a tuft of brown hair coming out of the top of her sleeping bag. Greta slept late. She worked hard at her dreams . . .

He dressed like lightning, before she could wake up and start talking. Once she started talking about her dreams, she'd go on for ever. Dad's fault. He took dreams seriously and would listen to her for ages, while his hands were making pottery.

Tobias slid the bus door open quietly and slipped out. The bus looked pearly grey with dew. It was green, really, with "PEACE" painted on the side where ordinary buses had the bus company's name. The bus was called Dylan. When Mum and Dad were young, it had been painted pink and blue, all swirls

1

and stars and Ban the Bomb signs. Mum had painted it herself, top to bottom, even if she was only five feet three. Sometimes bits of green paint got scraped off the bus, showing the bright pink still underneath. It was like discovering the past, in archaeology.

Dad had painted the bus plain green last year, because the pink and blue swirls caused the Fuzz to get stroppy. When he went into Lowestoft he got parking tickets when other people didn't. Mum still got angry about the re-paint sometimes. Once she'd cried about it. Dad told her to grow up.

The Fuzz still got nasty about the bus having "PEACE" painted on it. But Mum wouldn't give up "PEACE". Tobias often wondered why the Fuzz hated the word "PEACE" so much. Did they *really* prefer war?

Having escaped Greta, he stood shivering pleasantly and looking up the valley. It was a very small valley, only one long field surrounded by a high hedge. But it had a stream running down the middle of it, and the grass was green and lush, and in some rushy places your wellies sank in up to their tops. The farmer hadn't been able to plough it for wheat. That's why Dad got it cheap. To the farmer the valley was a nuisance, a break in his huge endless wheatfield. He'd have liked to rip out the hedge, as he'd ripped out all the other hedges for miles around, so they wouldn't get in the way of the combines. But the valley was swampy and useless, so the hedge stayed. It had lots of birds and hedgehogs and dragonflies from the stream. And fifty different kinds of plant. Willowherb and foxglove, nettles and docks. The nettles stung you, and the dock-leaves cured the sting, Mum said. The foxgloves, boiled, were good for your heart; but too many killed you. The willowherb was good for something, but he'd forgotten what.

Dad said every different plant in a hedgerow meant ten years; so the hedge must be five hundred years old.

The five white goats, on their pegged ropes, were further up the valley than they'd been last night. Mum must have moved them after she'd milked them. One was a billy-goat, useless for milk. But he'd been born in the valley, and christened Jack. He was one of the family and Mum couldn't bear to send him away to be killed. And he was getting bigger and nastier all the time. Dad often sighed about it, but nothing was ever done.

Nearer were the Rhode Island Reds, pecking the grass round their stong grey hut. Foxes came round every night who chewed and scrabbled at the corners of the hut door, but it was too strong for them. The cow was grazing among the chickens. They'd got her cheap, because she'd lost two calves in a row and was heading for the knacker's yard. She was an experiment. If she was loved enough, would she keep her next calf and give milk? And was there enough grass in the valley to feed her and the goats through the winter? She was very affectionate and called Daisy.

He walked across to the kitchen door. There were only two rooms in the cottage, the kitchen and the room where Mum and Dad slept. A puff of warm air hit him in the face as he walked through the door, making him break into a sweat even in the coolness of the morning. The Aga was on day and night, winter and summer, because it was their only way of cooking and getting hot water. It made the kitchen snug in winter, but hell in summer. In summer they ate outside on the grass, or in the bus if it was raining.

3

The kitchen was big, with a stone slab floor, a big scrubbed table and a pantry with stone shelves to keep things cool. There were old beams. Mum knocked nails into them and hung up bunches of herbs to dry, that tickled Dad's bald head as he passed. It was funny, Mum being so little and Dad so big: six feet four. It made Dad hard to talk to, except when he was sitting down, making pottery. Mum was easy to talk to, your own height, though she might give you a clout over the ear. Dad never hit anybody, even wasps. If a wasp got into the pottery he would catch it in a pot and put it out the door. Dad said all life was sacred; Mum said what about germs?

Mum was on the phone as usual this morning. She was a Labour councillor and did the "This is your right" column for the local free newspaper. She was always helping the underdog and on the phone to the bureaucrats, giving them hell. Like now.

"How much rent do you say these people owe?"

"Crackle, crackle," said the bureaucrat.

"Two hundred pounds? That's hardly a fortune!"
Crackle, crackle.

"You know the husband's been off work eight weeks with a slipped disc?"
Crackle, crackle.

"And if you put them out of their house, they'll have to go into board-and-lodging in Lowestoft. At council expense. Two hundred pounds a week! That hardly makes sense even by Thatcherite standards."
Crackle, crackle.

"Yes, of course I'm going to write about it in the *Clarion*. Don't you like people knowing what you're doing to people?"

The crackle sounded a lot humbler, suddenly.

"I'll talk to them," said Mum. "Will you accept

4

two pounds a week back-payment? Thank you!"

She didn't sound in the least thankful.

She said, without turning round "Egg on fried bread, Tobias?" and before he could answer, popped an egg in the pan. He always had egg on fried bread, fried in soya oil for health. They never had bacon; Mum had once had a pet pig . . .

Next minute she was back on the phone to somebody else. Dad said Mum was born with a frying pan in one hand and a phone in the other.

Tobias ate his egg quickly; the heat in the kitchen was getting terrible, in spite of the window being open. A wasp flew in and Mum swatted at it with the cooking-slice. It crawled away down the windowsill disconsolately, more oily than injured, and flew off.

Greta barged in in her floral nightdress, which she wore all day when it was hot, with no shoes. She was full of a dream about a marrow that grew as big as a house, while Mum continued to give the East Anglian Water Board hell about living creatures coming out of the cold water tap of a cottage in Beccles . . . the kitchen was like a madhouse.

Tobias fled to the peace of the pottery, which was at the back of the cottage. It was long and wide but rather low; it had once been a pig-sty. Even after three years, Dad still bumped his head at least once a day. Mum was always threatening to buy him a crash helmet.

It was cool in the pottery; stone slab floor again. The biggest electric kiln was switched on, its little red eye glowing, but it was only just starting to heat up. On top of it were rows of pots stacked to dry, waiting their turn in the kiln; no heat was wasted in a pottery. Dad was sitting dreamily at the pottery-wheel, centring a piece of wet clay, his long, long leg

5

smoothly rising and falling on the kick-wheel. Tobias watched his father's huge hands squeezing the clay; down into a mushroom shape, then up into a tower. Very wet clay, like grey cream, squeezed out between his fingers. He seemed to go on for ever, then suddenly he shoved his huge thumb down into the centre of the clay, and a tall pot grew up between his fingers like a flower opening in a nature film. Taller and taller, unbelievably tall and beautiful; all in one minute. Then Dad lifted it off the wheel and set it to dry, and fell to dreaming over another lump of whirling clay.

Dad was a man of clay; his smock was plastered with it, where he wiped his hands. It stayed there till it dried and cracked off and fell to the floor and was trampled to dust under his clayey shoes. He had clay on the handkerchief that stuck halfway out of his pocket, and clay on his nose from using the hand-kerchief, and clay in his beard and clay on his bald head and clay on his long hair that straggled down hippy-style behind. Dad spent nearly all his time in the pottery now, since the Anglia TV broadcast and the article in the *Observer*. Orders kept pouring in and so did the money. That's how they'd bought the valley. The'd lived in the bus in the commune until then and it was horrible in winter.

People liked Dad's big crazy leaning pottery clocks, and his sexy cats and the cockeyed houses with the tiny cat rubbing against the doorjamb. Dad was quite famous, and hated it; hated having to make up answers for people who came with tape-recorders and asked the same silly questions over and over. He hated leaving the valley to go up to London. He missed the long dreamy walks he had time for, before he got famous. But he liked not having to worry about money, except the Income Tax drove him mad.

Suddenly, he noticed Tobias standing there for the first time, and smiled and nodded to him in a friendly way, like an old man leaning on a gate watching the sunset. Tobias nodded back to him in exactly the same way. He liked to sit and watch for hours, nobody saying anything.

Unfortunately, after about ten minutes and another pot, Greta barged in full of her rotten marrow dream and then Mum came in as well. Mum and Greta were the noisy ones. Tobias got up to go, but Mum said to Dad, "You haven't forgotten we're off to Stonehenge on Friday? Is the bus ready?"

Dad sighed, picked up a modelling tool and stuck it viciously into his lump of clay. He went on digging the tool into the clay, not looking at Mum, and said, "I don't think I want to go this year."

"Why ever not?" Mum drew herself up to her full five feet three. Her long red hair, streaming free down her back, seemed to bristle. "We always go to Stonehenge for Midsummer."

"There was too much trouble last year. Too many people. The Fuzz got nervous. The farmers didn't like it. They've put a fence round Stonehenge . . ."

Mum went up like a rocket. She went up like a rocket at least ten times a day, but this was a real beauty.

"It makes me sick! These people who think they *own* Stonehenge. Putting fences round it, charging admission, selling their stupid little pamphlets. It's like fastening Stonehenge up in a zoo. Stonhenge doesn't belong to anybody. The people who made it have been dead three thousand years. Stonehenge belongs to the people who enjoy it, not silly old wazzocks in white nightshirts . . ."

7

For once, Tobias was on Mum's side. Every year he could remember, they'd gone to the Stones at Midsummer, to see the sun rise . . . to smell the smoke of the campfires. The closeness of the people, how everybody talked to everybody and there were no strangers but the straight people. You could run barefoot; you could run stark naked, and nobody bothered. And they sang the old songs, the Bob Dylan songs. And the Fuzz hung around the edges trying to arrest people, but they didn't dare because there were too many people and they were all one big family.

"Look," said Dad, "that Peace Convoy's getting out of control. Too many hangers-on who don't care, don't clean up the campsites, and peddle hard stuff. They don't wash and they make trouble. We just got away with it last year. And I've got so much work . . ."

Mum glared at him with her green eyes. "Work . . . bread . . . it's all you think about now. You're getting so *straight*. You'll be wanting us to get married next . . ."

Dad flinched as if she'd hit him. But she didn't care. She just said "Well, *I'm* going. Even if I have to drive Dylan myself." And she swept out.

Dad picked up his lump of clay and threw it back into the clay-bin. The dreaming light had gone out of his eyes; there'd be no more pots today.

Tobias wandered off miserably, thinking about the Fuzz. PC Johnson, who lived in the village was sort of okay. He was always dropping in for a cup of tea; nobody left Mum's kitchen without a cup of tea. PC Johnson loved to sit with Dad and talk about cars. He said everybody should buy a Ford or Austin Rover – the spares were cheaper. But you couldn't argue with him, or soon he'd be making out it was a crime not to buy Ford or Rover. The trouble with the Fuzz, they always had to be right. And when they got together in a crowd . . . Big crowds of Hippies just got happier. But big crowds of Fuzz . . .

Chapter Two

Everyone sat round the campfire, talking softly, so it was hard to hear above the crackle of the wood. A small night breeze swung the woodsmoke about, through every point of the compass. But they'd all grown up with campfires; they closed their eyes automatically as the sweet-smelling smoke engulfed them. The fire was old and nearly smokeless anyway: a mound of white ash that glowed and blushed suddenly and flamelessly as the breeze caught it, and sent scatters of miniature snowflakes of ash over their muddy boots stretched out to the heat.

Tobias was warm down his front and chilly down his back. That was always the way when darkness fell. He liked the difference of front and back. It made him feel shivery, alive, as he leaned back against Dad's knees.

Beyond the firelit faces, the old vans and buses were parked in a circle. Not to keep the wind out; nothing could keep the wind out. Not to keep the dark out; the dark was a friend.

It was keep the hate out. All day long they had driven through hate. Field-gates blocked with ploughs and tractors, that had once stood open and friendly. Groups of farmers who brandished shotguns as they passed. Shops that refused to serve them. People who would not tell them the way. It had all been so different, other years. Then there had been no helicopters buzzing in the sky, full of Fuzz or TV men pointing their cameras down at you, even when you stopped to pee behind a hedge.

Dad said the newspapers were whipping up the hate, because hate sells papers.

They had watched Chief Constables talking on Tom Blewett's portable telly. Saying that this year they would make an example. Acting big, with red beefy faces.

Make an example of whom? People who only wanted to be together and sing the old songs and watch the sun rise over the stones? What if they did drop a bit of litter, trample the odd turnip? That didn't cost a hundredth as much as all these helicopters and idle farmers were costing.

We'll be gone in three days, if you leave us alone. *We're* not killing the countryside with insecticides and combines and big new motorways and factories. We come and move on like the swallows, like the autumn leaves.

But you hate us because we're different. *We* don't make atomic bombs or kill whales or fill the sea with radioactive waste. We dare to be different, so you hate us. Tobias felt like crying. Why were straight people so full of hate? Why did they put up the "Closed" signs in cafés, when Dylan pulled up in the carpark? Isn't our money as good as yours?

11

Tobias had had three days of it, and his stomach felt sick. How must the gypsies feel, who suffered it all the time?

Above his head, Dad tried to speak calmly, tried to calm the others.

"What can they do? They can't touch us. All our vans are MOT'd and licensed. And trespass is a civil thing – they can only sue us in court, and by that time we'll be gone."

"The Pigs can always find something," said Tom Blewett. "Even if they have to go back to 1066. I tell you, the Pigs are plotting something, to please the straight people. They've not gone home tonight. They're still out there in their cars, muttering into their radios. They're excited . . . and you know what they're like when they get excited."

"I'm a British citizen," said Dad. "I pay my taxes. I haven't broken any law. What have I got to be afraid of?"

"Ask the Yorkshire miners," said Tom Blewett. "Ask the Greenham Common girls. They were all British Citizens too."

They talked on and on. If there was one thing Hippies could do, it was talk. They thought talk could solve all the problems in the world. Tobias began to feel sleepy; he nodded, dozed. But he didn't want to be alone in the bus, worrying about the Fuzz. There was safety being near people. He curled up like a dog, between Dad's feet and the ashes of the fire, and slept. Much later, he felt Dad's huge hands lift him up and carry him back to his sleeping bag in the bus. He didn't wake up; he trusted Dad not to drop him. He didn't take his clothes off; he was too scared to. He just crawled inside the soft warmth and fell asleep.

The first thing he heard was Tom Blewett shouting.

"They're coming! They're coming!" Tom sounded half-crazy with fear. Tobias leapt out of his bunk in the bus, all trembling and feeling sick and desperately trying to get the sleep out of his eyes so he could see properly. It was very early; before sunrise; grey light and mist still rising. And wading through the waist-high mist, from the road, came more Fuzz than he had ever seen in his life. In their short black raincoats and crash-helmets, with dark dogs like wolves. The worst thing about them was that you couldn't see their faces, behind their visors. The second worst was the truncheons they swung like swords in their hands. From the way they held them, you knew they *wanted* to use them.

The next thing he saw was Dad in the driving seat of the bus, desperately trying to start the engine. On the fourth attempt, the big engine chugged into life on about three cylinders. Dad wrestled the steering wheel backwards and forwards, and then they were slowly bumping over the tussocks towards the safety of the road at about five miles an hour, in bottom gear. Tobias saw the line of policemen part to let them through . . .

And then two of the biggest policemen leapt at the bus windscreen, swinging their batons at it. Dad stopped, to avoid running them down. The first blows of the truncheons bounced off the toughened glass. But the policemen kept on hitting at it, until it broke into a spiderweb of cracks. With the next blow, the fragments of glass flew into Dad's face. He cried out and put his hands to his face. He must have taken his foot off the accelerator, because the engine died.

Now the two policemen were walking down each side of Dylan. They were still hitting with their truncheons, smashing in pane after pane of glass. Bits flew everywhere: over Mum's cooking-stove, and the little table with the seersucker tablecloth, where they ate. Over the washing-up in the sink, over the bunk where Greta was still dreaming of her giant marrow. She suddenly woke up and began screaming her head off, as only a seven-year-old can. Mum grabbed her to her nightie, and held her tight.

Now two policemen were trying to force open the bus door, hammering on it with their truncheons. They didn't look like policemen usually do; they looked crazy, like kids when they're breaking glass bottles.

Dad lurched to his feet, blood, trickling down his face and getting lost in his beard. His eyes were still all squinted up, from the bits of glass in them; but he opened the bus door before the two policemen pulled it off its hinges. The policemen immediately reached in and dragged him down the bus steps, so he fell on the ground.

He picked himself up slowly and painfully, scrabbling with his hands. He turned to the policemen and said very calmly, rather sadly, "Friends, why have you smashed my bus?" Dad had been brought up as a Quaker. He always called strangers "friend", especially if they were hostile.

It was a mistake. It made the policemen even wilder. The bigger one raised his truncheon and hit Dad. He meant to hit him on the head; but Dad moved just in time, and the truncheon hit him on the shoulder instead. Dad fell down again.

Mum went berserk. She flew down the bus steps and leapt at the bigger policeman, hitting him in the chests with her tiny fists.

"Leave him alone, you bastards. What's he done to you?"

The policeman grabbed Mum's tiny fists in his huge ones. "You're under arrest. Get the cuffs on her, Alan." And in a second, Mum was handcuffed.

Tobias just stood there. He couldn't believe it was happening. A more important policeman came running up.

"What's going on here?"

"We're arresting her, sir. Assault."

"What about my kids?" yelled Mum. "You are going to arrest them too?"

For the first time, the important policeman looked worried. He was excited, but not wild like the other two. He was keeping his wits about him.

"They can go to relatives . . ."

"My relatives are two hundred miles away," said Mum, seeing her chance. "My father's a professor. In Cambridge."

The policeman studied her closely. The trouble was, Mum sounded posh. She tried very hard to hide it usually. But when she got upset she sounded very posh indeed. Dad always said that she wouldn't ever sound like a child of the workers in a million years.

Just then, a bit late, there was the sound of a helicopter in the sky. Everybody looked up. It wasn't a police helicopter. There was a man leaning out pointing a TV camera.

"Let her go!" shouted the boss policeman. "Let her go, you stupid bastards. Get those cuffs off her."

"But she bloody hit me . . ."

"Let her go. If you value your bloody job. I don't want any sob-stories in the press. What's the man charged with?"

"Drove this bus straight at us . . ."

"Attempted murder. Book him."

Dad was led away between the two policemen. He

15

kept stumbling on the tussocks; they had to hold him up. Mum walked behind, still yelling at the them.

Tobias looked around. The campsite was a shambles. There were only six vans and buses left, all with their windows smashed in. The rest seemed to have got away. But they'd left their stuff behind. Pans buckled and plates broken where buses had driven over them; tents and sleeping bags trampled flat and muddied by the Fuzz's feet. The people who'd had their vans smashed were just standing, paralyzed, helpless. They clutched belongings, a frying pan, a kid's anorak, as if they didn't know why they were holding them. A few dogs wandered about, sniffing things and looking lost.

But the oddest thing was the policemen. They looked bewildered too, like they were coming out of a dream. One young one stood staring at a carrycot that a bus wheel had gone straight over. Three more were banging each other on the back idiotically, as if they were footballers who'd just scored a goal. It was all so *unreal*.

The important policeman was coming back, still with Mum at his heels. Mum was still insisting that he arrest her. She was threatening him with her solicitor and half the city of Cambridge. "And what about my bus?"

"The bus is impounded," said the important policeman. "It wouldn't pass an MOT test. It's unfit to drive."

"We had it MOT'd two weeks ago!" yelled Mum.

"It's unfit because of broken windows. And it's required as evidence. It will be taken to the car pound at Walchester. Any enquiries should be made there. You have ten minutes to remove your possessions . . ."

"And how do I get these kids to Walchester?"

"You could try walking. Now excuse me . . ."

He strode off in a different direction.

Mum packed after fashion. Tobias could tell her mind wasn't on it. She'd pick up a tin of beans and stand staring at it for ages. But he didn't feel much better himself. Everything in the bus was all broken glass – the pans, the sleeping bags. It had begun to rain, and a wind was getting up, blowing the rain through the broken windows. The bus was still home, and yet it wasn't any more. Like your cat, when it's been run over and killed, isn't your cat any more, and yet it is.

Greta sat on her bunk, like a little rabbit crouching in her burrow, her eyes huge and her thumb in her mouth. She hadn't said anything since she'd stopped screaming. She kept staring at the policemen, who were waiting and watching outside. The policemen stared back with a sort of miserable contempt, as they might stare at a squashed and dying animal.

Tobias got his rucksac, and filled it with anything he thought might be useful. It was hard to decide, because he didn't know where they were going, and what was going to happen. But Dad's big torch would be useful . . . and he'd take Dad's little radio, because someone was bound to nick it. And a blanket. And Mum's cigarette lighter. And Dad's college scarf. He kept on wondering what the police were doing with Dad . . . Then he got Greta's duffle-bag and stuffed all her clothes into it.

By that time, Mum had made a huge bundle wrapped in polythene, with a bit of rope round it to carry it. The bundle was nearly as big as she was. Then she got dressed. The policemen were still staring in through the broken windows, so she just

17

pulled her jeans and her big Icelandic sweater and her anorak over her nightdress. She put on her green wellies, and then got Greta dressed. Greta held out her arms and legs on command, like a zombie. Then Mum staggered down the steps with her bundle. The very young policeman tried to help her down the bus steps, but she pulled her hand away, and gave him a look like a dagger.

Mum took one last look round the campsite, but there was no one left to say goodbye to, only one dog sniffing around. She shouldered her bundle and they set off towards Walchester. Tobias hadn't a clue how far it was. And the rain was getting heavier all the time.

They walked for three hours through driving rain. They were soaked through, and the wind cut like a knife. It wasn't like midsummer; it was more like November. Tobias' wet jeans began to chafe his legs on the inside. His trainers squelched, like he was walking in a bog. His hands were red and raw, where he tried to ease the weight of the rucksac cutting into his shoulders through the padding of his anorak.

Mum still plodded on ahead, like a beast of burden. Just a pair of green wellies under the great sodden pile of bedding still half-wrapped in the plastic sheeting that the wind tore at hungrily.

Greta plodded close behind her, to get some shelter from the awful wind, like a calf following a cow. First she'd grumbled, then she'd whined. Then she'd whimpered to herself and now she was silent, saving her breath to put one leg in front of the other. Every so often, she staggered a bit. Tobias would have liked to have helped her, but he was carrying her duffle-bag as well as his own rucksac and he hadn't a free hand. He'd tried telling her jokes at first, and then he'd tried singing, but she was past all that now, and so was he.

There seemed hardly any houses round here at all. Just a few big farmhouses set well back from the road, and their drives were blocked with tractors and ploughs. Tobias knew what kind of welcome they'd get if they tried there. They passed telephone boxes; but Mum had left her purse back in the bus, and Tobias only had a few coppers. Besides, Grandpa and Grandma weren't in Cambridge; they were off on an archaeological dig in Cyprus.

There were no buses; not that that mattered when they had no money. A steady stream of cars passed, each one spraying them with muddy water from the road. Faces watched them curiously through rain-spattered windscreens – men's, women's, children's. Faces eating sandwiches, chewing toffees. In the cars the heaters would be on, the radios playing; a different world.

Some of the faces in the cars looked hostile; some a bit sympathetic; most looked at them as if they were animals in the zoo. Curious, but only a bit curious. Not curious enough to stop, let alone offer a lift. People in cars never offer lifts to wet people; it might spoil their upholstery. Besides, they weren't just wet; they were the peculiar people who'd been causing all the trouble on the telly, the famous Hippy Convoy. A threat to law and order, not really a part of the human race.

Eventually, they came to the great big hill. The main road went up like a staircase. They'd *never* manage it. But another road forked off to the right that didn't look so steep. Head down, like a weary animal, Mum took the little road. They left the roar-roar of the cars behind; they weren't splashed any more. It was a relief.

But the little road was steep too. Tobias thought they would never get up; that their legs would simply stop walking halfway. It took for ever. And when they did get to the top, the wind hit them with double force.

Greta suddenly staggered, and fell down. She sort of slid down into the muddy ditch by the roadside. To Tobias' amazement, she simply curled up into a ball and went fast asleep. He leapt down into the ditch and shook her shoulder. She opened her eyes, smiled at him lazily and happily and said, "Leave me alone, Tobias. I'm just going to have a little nap." She put her head back on her hands and closed her eyes, that little smile still on her face.

It was so weird, there in the pouring rain, that he flew into a panic. Took her by both shoulders and shook her whole body. She muttered dreamily, "Leave me *alone* Tobias. Just a *little* nap."

He lifted her up bodily upright, but her legs were like rubber. She fell down again, pulling him on top of her.

"Mum!" screamed Tobias. "MUM!"

Mum went on plodding on; she hadn't heard.

"MUUUUUUUUUM!"

She turned, looking furious. Then her face went all frightened, and she dropped her bundle and ran back.

"What's the matter? Has she hurt herself?" Mum's chin was quivering; she was biting at her lip as if she really was trying to eat it.

"She says she wants to sleep. She keeps on falling asleep."

"Exposure," said Mum. "She's got exposure. If we don't get her somewhere warm quick, she'll die. I've seen it mountaineering."

Tobias had never heard of exposure. But Greta looked odd enough to die. He looked round desperately for a warm place. The only houses were far below, on the main road, looking as small as Monopoly houses. The only thing near was a low grey building across a field, that looked like a barn. The little windows were only black holes, and there seemed to be a few slates off the roof, but the door was open. And barns had hay or straw. Anyway, it was the only place.

Together, they picked her up and carried her somehow.

Chapter Three

The barn had great thick stone walls. There was a door, pushed back against the wall, huge and silvery oak, with great rusty iron hinges. Tobias had to use all his strength to force it shut.

The wind dropped to a shrill moaning. It felt a lot warmer, so he shivered, as he looked round in the sudden dark made by closing the door. Light came in only through a few narrow slits high up, and a few chinks in the roof at one end, but when his eyes got used to it, he could see quite well.

There was a pile of old straw that was dry. They got Greta on to it, and she promptly fell asleep again. But Mum quickly undid her great bundle of bedding and there were two towels inside, quite dry. They undressed Greta and rubbed her warm, and got her into dry jeans and jumpers, and the only dry blanket. Whereupon she came awake as bright as a button, only with a headache, and asked for something to eat. Tobias shouted she must have been pretending all the time; but Mum said exposure was like that. She was made to lie still, but given the last of the chocolate digestives.

Mum spread all the wet things around the straw to dry. "We could do with a long bit of rope to hang them on."

Tobias roamed round the barn, rummaging under the straw and in corners. He found a rusty sickle for cutting grass, in a hole in the wall.

"I hope the farmer doesn't come . . ." said Mum, very timid for her.

"Don't think anybody's been here for years," shouted Tobias. "Everything's totally rusty. There's nothing to come here *for*." Then he found something huge and spiky and heavy, under more straw in the far corner. "Hullo – what's this?" He dragged it towards the light. It scraped across the uneven stone floor, making a plantpot sort of noise. He began to pull the straw off it; the thing, whatever it was, seemed to stick out in all directions. Finally, he pulled it clear. It was the weirdest thing he'd ever seen.

At the bottom was a sort of pointed roof. On it stood a rough four-legged animal, made of tubes of fired clay. From its sticky-up ears, it might have been a model of a horse. Certainly there was a rider on its back, also made of rough tubes of fired clay. He had a crude wide-brimmed hat, two rather sticky-out eyes and sticky-out beard. He wore a belt, and stuck in the belt, a cross-shape that might have been the handle of a broken-off sword. In fact there were bits chipped off it all over the place, and it was blackened, as if with soot.

"What is it?" called Mum, as she sat by Greta.

"It's an old man on a horse." Tobias said it quick as

a flash. He only wondered afterwards how he was sure it was an *old* man on a horse. How he seemed to recognize it. Or did it recognize him?

For he knew from the start that it was magic. It had . . . life inside it. Like the brass Buddha Dad kept in the bedroom at home. Only much, much more magic than the Buddha. A grim, black, battered magic. He squatted back on his heels, wondering if it was evil. He wished he'd never found it. He would have liked to cover it up again. Pretend he'd never found it; but he had and he couldn't un-find it. Even if he covered it up again, he would know that it was there, and it would know that he was there.

He shivered; but that might only be because he was soaking wet.

"I wish you'd stop mucking about," called Mum crossly. "I wish there was some way of making a hot drink." Tobias looked at her, across the barn, where she huddled on the straw beside Greta. She looked so little; she looked . . . shrivelled and beaten. With her frying pan in one hand and the telephone in the other, she was a giant, but she didn't have them now. And looking at her, an awful despair filled Tobias' heart. The Fuzz had blown them apart. Dad in the nick somewhere. Poor smashed Dylan, somewhere else. Home and Daisy hundreds of miles away, through the pouring rain. Grandpa in Cyprus, going on digging in the sun, as if nothing had happened. All that was real was the cold stone walls of this place, the beating rain, the grey dripping miles outside. They were in a great wet cold prison, and there was no way out. It couldn't be happening. But it was.

There was no help, no power. Except in the blackened grim object before him. The old man on his horse. Again, he sensed the cold stony power in it.

He touched it. He whispered, "Help us. Help us." Then, "Make it all right." He knew he was being silly; that everyone he knew would have laughed at him. But a darker deeper part of him knew he wasn't being silly at all. He knew if it helped him, it would want something in return. It would want paying, like the hire-purchase firms Mum and Dad hated so much. And he didn't know what the payment would be; he didn't know which parts of him it would want.

Nothing seemed to happen. He grew restless and stared around the barn.

In the shadows, at the far end from the door they'd entered by, there seemed to be another door . . .

He forced back a rusted bolt. The door grated back, dragging on the floor. Light poured past him, into the darkened barn. He stepped into a new room.

He could tell straightaway it was a kitchen. Some-body's kitchen. There was a huge black fireplace nearly as big as a room itself, that you could stand up in. Inside it, from a long rusty arm, swung a black pot like a jam-pan. There was even a big fire of logs in place, ready to light. But there was no paper under the logs. Instead, there were shavings of wood and thin black twigs. He wondered if he could get it to light from Mum's cigarette lighter.

There were other things in this kitchen. A bench with a high back, all carved; the wood was very black and greasy. A huge table, with a row of burn-marks along one edge, and a row of deep chopping-marks along another. Funny way to treat a table! Mind you, it looked as if it could stand such treatment. The top was four inches thick, and so hard he couldn't even dent it with his fingernail.

In one corner, behind a low wooden wall, was a

great heap of rough-chopped logs; in another corner a pile of old planks set upright. In a third, a stone sink with a water-pump made out of a whole treetrunk.

But the oddest thing was that nobody could've been here for years. Spiders' webs ran all over the place; whole spider palaces higher than he was, fattened up with dust and the sucked-dry transparent bodies of dead flies. And the inch-thick grey carpet that deadened his footsteps and tore as he walked on it was not a carpet at all – it was grey dust. He coughed, as the dust filled his lungs; retched as if he was going to be sick. It felt like he was suffocating in a tomb. Frantically, he tore the cobwebs off the small window.

Outside, it looked just the same; an endless succession of humpy-backed grey hills, fading one behind the other into the grey rain.

"Tobias? What are you up to?"

He went back to explain.

This was better. Mum had found a broom of long black twigs, and she attacked the cobwebs and the dust as if they were the policemen back at the campsite. In an hour, the place was spotless. Tobias had managed to get the fire going with Mum's lighter and several crumpled up Greenpeace anti-whaling pamphlets nicked from Mum's handbag. A fire of huge logs roared like a lion up the chimney; Tobias had never seen such fat hungry flames.

They were warm and dry – alive again.

Tobias had worked the handle of the pump like a fury, and at last dark ivy-smelling water had come out. There was an odd wobbly cockeyed bucket that was as hard as iron, but turned out from its smell to be leather.

Greta was huddled under the blanket on the high-backed bench that Mum called a settle, by the fire. But she was moaning that she was hungry again. And Mum was swearing because although she'd brought three tins of beans and a tin of corned beef, she'd forgotten the tin opener.

Tobias looked out of the small kitchen window. The rain had stopped. It was a fine night, with the moon riding high through some last streaks of rain cloud.

"I'll see what I can do Mum," he said.

"What d'you mean – see what you can do?"

"Find something to eat . . ."

"I'll not have stealing!"

"Don't worry." He slipped out before she could argue. He couldn't get the new kitchen door to the outside open, so he slipped back through the barn.

The night wind was cold, and nibbled through his clothes where they weren't quite dry yet. But it was great to be out alone in the dark. He felt wild and free, like a fox, as he worked down the hedgerow. He seemed to have left the daylight Tobias behind altogether. The Tobias who must not steal. Dad would never steal; he'd let people steal from him, if they were poor and took no more than they needed. Mum would never steal, though she said the straight capitalist world stole from people all the time. But other boys in the Hippie convoy stole. And Tobias had gone with them on their stealing trips, and learnt how to do it. And the Fuzz had stolen Dad's bus. And since the Fuzz were doing what Mrs Thatcher wanted, and the Queen hadn't stopped them either, then everybody was a thief. What good was Dad's honesty, when he got a faceful of glass? What good was Mum's honesty, when Greta nearly died of exposure? Nobody was going to help them. Granny said God helped those who helped themselves. Foxes helped themselves . . . And he was hungry, and Mum and Greta were hungry, and they had only him, to look after them.

He came to a gap in the hedge. Far off, down in the valley, the lights of motorcars followed each other like a moving chain down the road. There were the red and gold lamps of farmhouse windows. But up here, where the humps of the hills were bathed in gentle moonlight, was an older world. He practised moving silently, although there was no one about. His ears took in every rhythm of the wind, through the hedge, through the corn, through the long grass at the side of the corn. He took a few heads of corn and rubbed out the grains between his palms and chewed them. They were green and juicy and bitter-sweet, but they started up a boiling hunger-ache in his belly that drove him on.

The field beyond the hedge was potatoes, in humped ridges with fine bushy tops. He didn't attack the first row; the farmer would notice. He went six rows in, planting his feet carefully between the ridges so as not to disturb the soil. And he didn't disturb the bushy potato-tops, but dug into the ridge from the side, through the loose soil. Six inches in, his hand closed round the first round potato, tangled up in its wiry roots. As big as an egg; the juices in his stomach went mad, as he drew it out, feeling the roots snap. One, two, three he drew out, then patted the soil gently back in place and went on to the next plant. If you took too many from one plant it died and the farmer would notice.

He filled his anorak pockets, and retreated back down the row, riffling up the flattened soil of his footprints with his fingers. He left the potatoes in a little pile by the gap in the hedge, where he could find them easily in the dark. He prowled on.

Found a field of turnips. Again, he went well out into the middle of the field. Took five small turnips, that the farmer would think were failures, well apart, and filled up the holes that they left. He left the leaves on to carry them by, and because dying leaves thrown in the hedge would alert the farmer in the morning. He didn't know how many times he would have to come back for more . . . Again he left them by a gate, to pick up later. He was walking towards the farm. If the farmer caught him, he wanted to have empty hands and empty pockets.

He approached the farm buildings with the wind blowing in his face. That way, the farm dogs wouldn't scent him and start barking. He didn't want to get shot for a fox. He was looking for hen huts, free range hen huts.

At the second farm, he found them. Old, grey, sagging, but full of the faint clucking of hens. He was doubly careful now. Hens were sharper than dogs; once they heard you and sent up their racket . . .

Of course, there was no hope of getting eggs from nest boxes in the huts without all hell breaking loose. But there were always bloody-minded hens who laid their eggs in hidden nests in the hedgerow; and often farmers were too lazy or busy to search for them.

He searched a long time in the moonlight. Just as he was despairing, he found a clutch of six eggs. Some might be rotten, of course, from lying in the sun. He stored them in the hood of his anorak, well-padded with grass. He didn't want egg yolk running down his back.

Content, he turned for home. It was then he had

his biggest stroke of luck. He saw Brer Fox before Brer Fox saw him. Mind you, it *was* pure luck. Luck that he was moving down-wind of the fox; luck that he was walking through loose soil that muffled his footsteps like a blanket. Luck that he wasn't moving uphill yet, with puffing breath. Luck that a wet anorak doesn't crackle.

Brer Fox pushed his head out of the hedge, almost at Tobias' feet; flashed him a terrified glint of eyes, green in the moonlight like mirrors, and was gone.

But Brer Fox had dropped something from his mouth that was white and floppy. A well-grown pullet, with its head bitten off, still warm and oozing blood. Perhaps the bold layer of eggs in the hedge had been bold once too often. He hoped not; they might need more eggs.

He picked up the potatoes and turnips and walked home well satisfied. He walked back into the kitchen with a swagger, and laid the things one by one on the table.

Mum was silent. With her head down, she stared at the things for a long time. For a terrifying moment, he thought Mum was going to make him take them back.

Then Greta wailed, "Aw Mum, I'm *hungry*!"

Finally Mum said, "When things are back to normal, we'll come back and pay the farmer." She reached for the little nest of aluminium camping pans.

They had chicken stew, with potatos and turnips. Tobias thought nothing had ever tasted so good, especially when a renewed tempest hurled itself against the window.

Chapter Four

Tobias slept late; his sleeping bag was still damp, though warm, and he was sleeping on the top of the big table with Mum, to avoid draughts that cut in under the kitchen door. He was a bit scared of rolling over in his sleep and falling to the floor. And the wind had talked round the house all night, making quite different noises from the ones it make talking round the bus.

But the fire was still alive, in its bed of white ash, and Mum had the big pot full of boiling water, and they had Nescafé without milk, and were able to have a wash with a sliver of soap.

Outside, the sky was patchy with rain clouds, though it wasn't raining at the moment. Mum said she wouldn't have any breakfast; she would try to hitch into Walchester, to find out what had happened to Dad and the bus. They would stay in the warm and dry, because Greta had a nasty cough and could hardly put one leg in front of the other.

After Mum had gone, it was awfully quiet, apart from the wind. Tobias kept himself busy, to keep out the quiet. He hung all the sleeping bags over the settle to dry off properly. He roasted some potatoes in the ashes and they ate one hard-boiled egg between them. Two of the eggs had turned out rotten.

It was a long, long day, with only the fire to keep them cheerful. He'd have liked to have gone out foraging for more grub but Mum had told him to stay put or she'd wring his neck. And Greta was terrified of being alone in this place. He had no watch; he couldn't even tell the time by the sun, because it stayed behind the clouds.

In the end, it began to get dark. He tried kidding himself it was only the thickening rain clouds. He went more and more often to the barn door, to look for Mum, but there was no sign of her, only distant cars passing very seldom on the road across the field. In the end, when the cars began to put their headlights on, he had to admit it was getting dark. He wondered about stopping a car and asking for help. But even if the people in the car were kind, they'd want to take him and Greta away from the barn. And then Mum would come back and find them gone, and everything would be worse. He and Greta might be handed over to social workers, and he'd heard Mum too often fighting her battles down the phone at home to have a high opinion of social workers. They took children away from their parents and put them in a home. They might bring a court case against Mum for leaving them alone in the barn . . .

On his last journey out through the barn, he sort of sensed the old man on the horse sitting in the shadows, watching him. Slowly, reluctantly, he went across to it, knelt down in front of it, felt its stony

32

coldness. He thought, to be fair, that he had asked for help, and the old man hadn't let him down. He'd given them the kitchen, and the fire, and the potatoes and eggs and chicken.

"Thank you," he said, very solemnly. Perhaps the old man wasn't *very* powerful; perhaps he had given what he *could* give. Perhaps he couldn't do big things like fetching Mum and Dad and the bus back.

"Can you . . . help us again?"

In the dim light of Dad's torch, the old man glared at him with stony sticky-out eyes and jutting beard. It seemed to be some sort of answer.

Anyway, Greta was yelling out for him, in near panic, so he went back to her. He made up the fire really big, so it lit the whole room, driving back the night to the window. He let Greta get back into her dry sleeping bag, having taken her outside for a widdle, gave her a cup of Nescafé and a boiled egg, and put the last of the potatoes in the ashes to roast. At least she stopped whinging and snivelling for Mum. Tobias' eyes roved around the room nervously; the wind was making the place full of creaks again; especially, it seemed, creaks coming through the low beamed ceiling. Almost as if somebody was walking about up there. What if there was another room overhead, and somebody was in it?

Anyway, he comforted himself, stretching out his trainers to the blaze, if there was somebody up there, they had no means of getting in here. Four thick stone walls, a ceiling unbroken by any trapdoors, a stout door that wouldn't even open from the inside, and a window too small for anyone but a child to crawl through. And he had shot the rusty bolt on the door that led to the barn.

Again he had an impression of footsteps overhead.

Footsteps moving to and fro, as if . . . getting something ready. He glanced at Greta. She was fast asleep. A day of fretting and the sudden snugness of fire and sleeping bag had sent her off. He was glad she wasn't awake to be scared; and yet it made him feel lonelier. His eyes roved restlessly . . . *was* there no way in? And then he saw the gap in his defences.

The planks in the corner. What was behind the planks piled up in the corner? Suddenly quivering, he tiptoed across the room. Began moving the planks aside as quietly as he could. The first three planks he moved revealed the beginnings of a door. A very old door, carved with panels that Dad would have called linenfold. God, that *was* old. Seventeenth century or earlier.

Suddenly, their safe place was a trap. He desperately tried to work out a way to bar the door with the planks.

But the door opened outwards. There was no way to bar it.

He could see the iron handle . . . he could wriggle under the planks and open the door a bit and listen.

He wriggled under, and turned the handle with a dry squeak, and opened a crack of darkness and listened.

He could hear nothing but the wind. He opened the door a bit more. He could just see, by the faint light of the fire, steps – narrow wooden stairs leading upwards and twisting to the left. And he smelt a smell. The tantalizing, stomach-churning smell of frying bacon. Somehow, it was soothing. If there was a person up there, they were *cooking*. He couldn't quite think that a murderer would be cooking. He crept silently in a little further; began to climb the stairs on his hands and knees, careful not to make the boards creak. He went round a corner, looked up, and at the top of the still-twisting stair, saw a dim golden glow that could only be candlelight.

And again, candlelight seemed a *kind* thing. So he crawled to the top of the stairs. A thick panelled door was half-open, letting out the candlelight.

He lay a long time now, all ears and nose, his skin almost twitching with concentration. No sound but the wind, no smell but frying bacon. And that most precious sense that tells you if there's somebody or nobody in a room.

He became convinced there was nobody. He got up, alarming even himself with his certainty, and pushed back the half-open door and slid into the room.

It was big – as big as the kitchen and as low as the kitchen, with similar beams across the ceiling. There was a much smaller fire burning, of tiny sweet-smelling logs that he thought might be apple wood. Two heavy old wooden chairs were set each side of the fire, with dark red velvet cushions on their seats. A long chest stood under the window, with carvings of faces inside arches, faces that seemed to twist in the firelight.

But most of the room was taken up with a huge curtained bed. That gave him a fright, till he found the bed was empty. Rumpled, but empty. And a huge pair of boots by the bed, one upright and one lying on its side. As if somebody big had just stepped out of them. The boots had huge square toes, and turned-over in flaps of leather at the top. The hangings of the bed were very blackened by what looked like soot, but they were woven with twisting golden animals and serpents. There was a table by the bed, and on it a short fat candle throwing up a long flame.

Sadly, it was from this flame that the smell of frying bacon came. It must be a tallow candle, made from the fat from fried bacon. Tobias' stomach felt very disappointed.

He sat on the bed, not knowing what to do, almost *wishing* that somebody would come. But he sat a long time and nobody came. Then he noticed yet another door. It had a huge lock, and a huge iron key in the lock. Almost as if he was being invited to turn the key and lock the door and be safe. He got up and locked it, with a sense of disappointment. But he understood. He was being helped again. The bedroom had been got ready for them to sleep in. The owner of the boots had lit the fire, lit the candle, and gone.

He examined the bed. For an ex-hippy, Mum was very fussy about beds – if they were clean and dry. This one, though rumpled, had thick clean sheets that smelt deeply of lavender. The mattress was a mountain of feathers, into which his knees sank deeply and softly. There was a huge feather bolster, and feather pillows. The feathers' ends came through and prickled a bit, but it would be a dream to sleep in, after the kitchen table last night.

"Oh, Tobias, you *are* clever." The voice made him jump. But is was only Greta in the doorway, thumb in her mouth. "You are clever. A *real* bed. A *real* candle. Really *cosy*." She curled up in the bed with a sigh of luxury, and fell instantly asleep again.

He tried to stay awake, on guard and sitting up. But the bed proved too sweet for him, and he too slept. His last thought was that he would love some bacon.

"Tobias, Tobias, come quick!" Greta was shaking him violently by the shoulder. The prickle of feather-quills and the smell of lavender reminded him he was

36

in a strange bed, and he came awake with a panicky rush that made his heart thump painfully. But she was excited, not frightened.

"There's *breakfast*. Downstairs. Hot." Then her face went sad. "Only someone's murdered a poor pig."

He jumped up gladly and ran down the stairs, thinking Mum had come back with Dad and everything was all right again.

But there was nobody about. Only the fire was blazing in its deep bed of ash, there were new things on the table, and an overwhelming smell of fried bacon and, even better, baking bread.

"Look at the funny plates. They go *boing*." She tapped a dull grey plate, huge and thick but full of dents, and it duly gave out a dull "boing". Tobias knew from what Dad had told him that the plates were called pewter, and most pewter plates were antique, though he'd never seen one so battered. But what interested him more were the great chunks of fried bacon, half an inch thick and swimming in clear fat. And the large loaf of bread that lay beside them, still warm to the touch. A healthy bread Mum would have approved of, dark brown in colour and full of great grains.

"Let's have it while it's hot," he said, as calmly as he could. He kept on glancing round nervously, feeling like Goldilocks and the Three Bears, but his screaming tummy was king.

Eating wasn't easy. There were no forks, only blunt knives with points, like the sort Boy Scouts had, huge and hard to hold. The loaf of bread buckled in under his hand as he tried to cut it. He managed to carve off chunks rather than slices.

"Is this butter?" asked Greta, putting a filthy finger into a rough mountain of pale yellow greasy stuff that kept oozing clear liquid from every crack, and stood in a pool of liquid on the plate.

It was. The best butter he'd ever tasted. Very salty. The bacon was very salty too, but marvellous. You had to hold a lump down with your hand on the greasy plate and saw a smaller bit off with the knife and put it in your mouth and chew and chew.

It was hard work; they must have chewed for half an hour in silence, till they were full to bursting.

"What's in the jugs?" mumbled Greta, her mouth still full and grease running down her chin. There were two big battered pewter jugs, and two pewter half-pint pots with handles.

He picked up the first jug, and sipped at it gently. His hands were so slippery with grease he nearly dropped it. The contents were a clear brown, strong-smelling and very bitter. He spluttered and said "I think it's beer."

"Uuuuurgh!" said Greta with disgust. "Fancy drinking *beer* for breakfast."

The other jug was creamy milk. She drank a lot of that, and wiped the milky moustache from her upper lip with her cuff. Greta went back to the wild pretty quickly, Mum always said, if she wasn't watched . . .

It was then that they heard the shouting outside. Men shouting. Big rough voices, excited, triumphant. For some reason they reminded Tobias of the Fuzz, back at the campsite. He ran to the kitchen window, and peeped cautiously over the sill.

"Men on horses. Six of them."

"*Fox-hunting?*" Greta hated fox-hunters more than anything. Somebody had once given her a pet fox cub she'd called Ferdy, but it grew up and wandered off. She still had days she spent wandering in the field at home, calling for Ferdy to come home . . .

"No. Not fox-hunters. They're dressed funny. Leather coats with no sleeves. *Metal* hats . . . *swords* – on sort of slings round their shoulders. Big *boots*." He tried hard to stop his voice going up into a childish squeak, like Greta's. Then he said, sounding disgusted, "Oh, they must be those silly people in the colour supplements. The ones who play at soldiers and Oliver Cromwell. The Tied Knot or something . . ."

"Who's Oliver Cromwell? Is he in *EastEnders*?" Greta had a deplorable taste for telly in general, and *EastEnders* in particular. Mum and Dad refused to have telly in the house. It meant that at the end of most days Dad had to go the rounds of the neighbours' cottages, asking if Greta was with them watching telly. It was the principal cause of World War III at home.

"No, stupid. Oliver Cromwell's in history. He fought against King Charles the First and cut his head off."

"D'you think he cut our pig's head off?"

"*What* pig?"

"The murdered pig. Somebody cut its head off, and hung it in the corner. *Look*!" She came and grabbed his shoulder, and pointed into the darkness of a corner of the larder.

There, from a hook in the ceiling, hung a very large half-pig, minus its head.

"No, stupid. That's a side of salted bacon. That's what we had for breakfast. They have them in the butcher's shop in Beccles."

"Oh. Poor pig. Tobias, I feel *sick*. And Mum says you're not to call me stupid . . ."

"Shut up. I'm watching these men; they're chasing cows about, trying to catch them. I'm sure they shouldn't. I'm sure it'll curdle their milk."

39

"I'm just sorry for the pig, that's all. And I *still* feel sick."

"Look, here's some more men coming. They've got a big cart with four wheels. It's full of sacks of stuff. And live chickens tied in pairs by their legs. Greta – I think they're stealing off the farms. They're stealing all the cows and chickens. Oh, God, they're coming over here now . . . quick! Hide."

He looked around wildly. The little low door into the barn seemed the best. It was dark in there. They could hide under the straw . . .

Tobias poked his head out of the pile of straw, and took a deep breath and sneezed violently. He'd spent the last twenty minutes trying not to sneeze.

He'd not seen a thing, but he'd heard a lot. Someone shouting outside in a great rough voice. Shouting something about "Parliament" of all things. Then there'd been a huge hammering on wood, a splintering that he had a good idea was the kitchen door giving way. Then there was a trampling of many feet, and voices that sounded like Dorset voices, though he couldn't make out a word they said. There'd been a dull clonking, like pewter. There'd been feet on the stairs and overhead, in the bedroom. But nobody had come into the barn. They must have seen it was empty.

Then the footsteps had faded away, then the voices outside. He listened a last time, heard not a thing, and jumped up, knocking the straw off himself, and ran back into the kitchen.

The kitchen door was gaping wide. Across the field, men were lifting things into the four-wheeled cart.

"That's our murdered pig," said Greta indignantly

over his shoulder. "What we going to eat now? And that's our mattress from upstairs . . ."

"They must be *lunatics*," said Tobias. "Pretending to be Tied Knot and stealing in broad daylight, and trying to get away in a horse and cart. Somebody'll report them, and the police cars will catch them in *minutes*."

"They've taken all the plates and all. And the bacon, and the bread and milk. There's nothing *left*!" She started to snivel. "What we going to have for dinner?"

But Tobias wasn't listening. He watched the cart and the cows and the men on horseback moving away. And then . . . it was just as they were crossing the crest of the hill, so he couldn't see properly. But it seemed to him that another bunch of men came galloping in from the left. At first he thought they were joining the first party. But they came in too fast; at such a gallop that they were bound to crash into the others. He thought he saw arms pointing, and flashes, and heard a sound like fire crackers. And more shouting and a quite dreadful scream. One man seemed to throw his arms up and start to fall off his horse.

And then they were all gone over the hill.

Only leaving one odd memory. The shape of the man who had led the charge, black against the sky. A man with a floppy hat and jutty nose and jutty beard.

Just like the old man on the horse.

It was all very baffling. He did what he could. He shut the smashed door, and managed to wedge it solid. It wasn't badly harmed; some of the stonework at the side had given way. He made up the fire – at least they could still keep warm. Greta retired back into her sleeping bag, having made sure that all the bedclothes upstairs had gone. She thought it was funny that nobody had stolen their own things, like the sleeping bags. But Tobias reckoned they were so old, they weren't worth nicking.

Either that, or it was all a *game*. This Tied Knot lot, he'd read in the supplements, took their games very seriously. They spent thousands of pounds on their copies of guns and armour and cannons. Maybe they spent money on the pewter pots and sides of bacon and feather beds and cows, just so they could nick them off each other . . . Maybe the bedroom upstairs hadn't been meant for him and Greta, nor the breakfast. Maybe they were just caught up in the middle of this game and nobody had noticed they were there. It seemed the only sensible explanation, though it didn't seem *very* sensible. But then, the things grown-ups got up to . . . maybe the hippy convoy was really some sort of game, and being a member of the Fuzz was a game too. Maybe all adults were just crazy . . .

Chapter Five

He was desperately worried about Mum. He went to the door of the barn. The rain was chucking it down again. The odd car passed, going along the road at the far side of the field. But none of them stopped.

"It's sunny outside," said Greta from her sleeping bag. "Can we go for a walk, Tobias? We might find something to eat."

He looked out through the kitchen window. The sun was shining brightly. The tops of the green hills looked inviting. He was sick of mouldering in this old house. Maybe if he got outside, he'd feel better. And at least Greta wasn't whinging . . .

"C'mon, then." He held out his hand to her. Pulled back the damaged kitchen door.

It was nice. Everything smelt terribly fresh after the rain. The sun was warm on their backs. Life wasn't as bad as all that . . . They followed the deep ruts that the cart had left in the field. There were birds chirruping and calling.

"There's one of those men," said Greta.

Tobias gave a nervous jump.

"No, it's all right," said Greta. "He's just lying down having a nap. Expect he's tired, playing at soldiers."

And indeed the man did look very peaceful, lying on his back with his legs stretched out. He wore the same kind of square-toed big boots as they'd seen in the bedroom. They must all have them.

They were only about twenty yards away, tiptoeing up to have a peep, when something made Tobias stop.

The man was too still. Not like a man asleep, but like a tailor's dummy lying on its back in a shop window. His chest didn't seem to be going up and down. And there was a buzz of flies. And . . .

Tobias clapped his hands sharply. Three crows that had been pecking in the long grass around the man, half-hidden, took fright and flew away.

"Stay here, Greta. I won't be a minute."

"Not without you . . ."

"*Stay*!" Something in his voice made her shut up and obey.

He went forward reluctantly. When he was two yards away, the flies fled too, with an angry final buzz.

The man's metal hat had fallen off, and lay on the grass, about a yard from his head. He had short light-brown hair, but his head was turned away, looking down the hill. Reluctantly, Tobias walked in a great circle, until he could see his face.

It was young and chubby. There was only a thin fuzz of whiskers on his chin. He must have been quite young, but his mouth was open, showing horribly blackened teeth. His brown eyes were open, watching Tobias. They looked surprised and sad.

44

Then two bluebottles settled back on to his face and he didn't twitch, and Tobias knew that he was dead. The Tied Knot wasn't playing a game; or the game had gone horribly wrong.

Tobias ran back to Greta.

"We must get back to the house. It's going to rain."

He grabbed her by the hand and hurried her towards the house.

Then stopped dead.

Round the open door of the kitchen, more of the Tied Knot were standing, holding horses. Their way back was cut off.

He got Greta into the nearest hedge for cover. The hedge was a comfort – high and deep, full of little dark caves they could duck into if anybody came. Full, too, of the old familiar plants: nettles and dock, foxgloves and willowherb. But once in its shade, he couldn't think what to do next at all. One part of him wanted to run to the men at the farm and tell them about the dead man. But another part didn't trust the men. They were so violent and rough and you couldn't make out what they said; they stole things and got killed. They were *weird*, like the Fuzz had been at the campsite. At home, you knew what rules grown-ups worked by; but here . . .

Greta soon got bored with sitting in the cave in the hedge. She began grumbling she was hot and hungry. Then she wanted to go to the loo. He had to give her his handkerchief to use this time. He got desperate to know what was *happening*. He poked out his head, left and right. On the left, the men had disappeared, but the horses were still standing round the farmhouse door. To the right, the land rose to the crest of a little hill. If they could creep up to the top, using the hedge for cover, he would be able to see a lot more of what was going on.

Greta grumbled all the way up. The worst bit was when they came across the cart. It was still full of sacks and squawking chickens tied together by their legs, their white wings fluttering. But the horse was lying on the ground between the shafts, and he knew it was dead. And there were at least three men lying round it, including the driver who was doubled forward on the cart seat. Tobias was just thankful the whole thing was quite a long way away from the hedge.

"Look," said Greta. "More men. Are they asleep too?"

"Yes," he said desperately. "It's a very tiring game they play."

"Yes," she said. "And the horse is tired too. And those two cows further up."

He gave up trying to work out what was going on. He knew modern soldiers sometimes got killed in military exercises in Germany, but the Tied Knot were just civilians, playing, doing it for fun. Some terrible accident; he supposed they'd read about it in the papers, eventually.

They reached the hilltop. He made her stay in the hedge "to keep cool and rest". She was hot and tired and didn't argue, though she grumbled the flies were biting her arms and legs. He stepped out, cautiously. There was no one nearby. He had got his good view; he could see a long way.

A quarter of a mile below, he could see the barn – or rather, farm. For the barn was just the end of a great long, low, straight building. He picked out the kitchen window, and door, and the bedroom

46

window above. But the farm went on and on beyond that.

He looked further, at the little road, and wrinkled up his brow. The little road looked different from here. It looked ragged and whitish-brown, like a track, whereas he knew it was really straight and neat, and the grey of tarmacadam. He couldn't see the white line that should be running down the middle. He couldn't see the black-and-white posts there'd been on either side, to help drivers in snow or mist. He couldn't see any telegraph poles, though he knew there'd been some . . . and no cars passing. No cars at all. Odd. It must be a Sunday or something. *Was* it Sunday?

He looked further, back down into the valley, to the main road. No cars passing there, either . . .

And then he saw it. Like a long railway train, moving terribly slowly. Or more like an enormous caterpillar, for it had hundreds of legs. Or a giant snake, because it was so long and so winding.

A gigantic column of men. In the front, horsemen. Kicking up white dust that hung around them, then drifted sideways across the fields, like smoke carried by a breeze. Glints came through the dust – the men wore metal hats and they had metal on their chests. The first horsemen carried a flag with a forked end. Black, with a white Maltese cross on it.

Hundreds of horsemen, riding two by two.

But behind, marching four by four, there were far more men on foot. Broken up into blocks like railway carriages, with big square flags in between, so big that the men carrying them staggered as the breeze hit them and the flags rippled. All the marching men carried long poles or short fat poles. The ends of the poles glinted. Most of the marching men seemed to have bare arms, for the heat. All the bare arms swung together. *Thousands* of them.

Then behind, cannons, great big old cannons pulled by strings of cows. And after that, huge wagons pulled by more strings of cows.

Then more horsemen. And then the end of the great snake vanished from sight, round the corner of the hill. God, it must be *miles* long.

Even the Tied Knot from all England couldn't have as many men as this. They were blocking the main road, so cars couldn't get past. The Fuzz would never allow that. Even on a Bank Holiday. Especially on a Bank Holiday!

Tobias gave a whimper. He knew then that he and Greta weren't just in the wrong place.

They were in the wrong *time* as well.

Lost in the middle of Cromwell's War.

He might have stood there for ever, paralyzed, if he hadn't noticed the horses had gone from round the farmhouse door.

It was their only chance, to get back to the right time. He took it.

He ran Greta so fast down the hill she had no time to be nosy about the men she thought were asleep. He dragged her so hard her feet left the ground three times. She would have fallen, but he sort of dragged her up and on again, so she didn't hurt her knees.

He ran her through the broken door just praying there'd be nobody inside. Lucky for him, there wasn't. Just the lingering smell of the lovely cooking. He slammed the broken door and wedged it shut with planks. Then he ran through the darkness of the barn and looked out the barn door.

On the distant road, a Currys' electrical van passed in the rain, its headlights glinting in the downpour.

48

They'd got back. His whole body turned to jelly with thankfulness.

When he'd stopped panting and shaking, he made up his mind that they weren't going through *that* again. He went back into the kitchen and grabbed all their own stuff, and carried it through to the barn. Then he grabbed Greta and hauled her through, despite her protests at leaving the lovely fire. Then he dragged shut the door between barn and kitchen – that seemed the very door of time itself – and wedged it shut with everything he could lay his hands on.

Greta crawled back into her sleeping-bag, on the straw. She moaned a bit, then fell asleep. The dark barn was infinitely dreary without her chatter. He could hear the rain thudding on the stone slates of the roof. It was raining here; in that other world beyond the barred door, the sun was shining brilliantly. There was warmth, the chance of food. But men died and lay unburied in that brilliant sun, with flies crawling on their surprised faces.

He felt, in the dark, the presence of the old man on the horse. Aware of them, watching them with stony eyes that never slept. It was all *his* doing, *his* dark magic. Tobias vowed he would never ask the old man for anything ever again. The old man charged too high a price.

But Tobias was greatly afraid he had asked him for too much already.

Then, greatly afraid still, he fell asleep. As men do, in the very presence of their enemies, after the tension of battle.

He was woken up by Greta's urgent hand on his shoulder; came awake with a terrible jump. But she was jubilant.

49

"Tobias! They've left us bread and lovely stew! Come and help me – it's too big an' hot."

He saw aghast what she had done while he was asleep, the little cow. Unbarred the door, led by the delicious smell and her never-satisfied belly. That belly of hers could get them both killed . . .

But he listened, and there was no sound but the pummelling of the rain on the barn roof. Night in the barn, and night in the kitchen. Through the barn door, he saw a late car pass on the road, reassuringly. Through the door into the kitchen, a dim glow.

Three tallow candles burning, giving off that smell of bacon. And the big pot hanging over the fire in the fireplace, gently bubbling with a dark brown stew full of lumps of meat and turnip. There were pewter dishes again, and a jug of milk.

Suspicious still, he prowled upstairs. The feather mattress and rumpled bedclothes were back on the bed. But there was a dark red stain on the coverlet, that was still damp to his touch. He smelt the metallic smell of blood, not properly washed out.

They would not sleep in *that* bed again!

But the stew and the milk and the still-fresh bread were too much to resist. Especially now he knew where to run to, if the men came back. Keeping a wary ear cocked to the kitchen door, he ladled out great lashings of stew into the deep plates.

It was smashing.

But they went back out into the cold damp barn to sleep. And he barred that door again.

Chapter Six

It was again Greta who shook him out of sleep. And again the damnable door was unbarred, with sunlight streaming through.

"There's a lady in the kitchen, cooking. She's a bit pongy and she speaks funny because she hasn't got many teeth, but she's very nice. She's going to let me bake bread."

Tobias walked through the door as wary as a cat. One look at the woman's dark grey dress that swept the dusty floor, and the soiled white linen bonnet that covered her ears like a helmet, told him that no help had come from the modern world.

The woman bobbed to him, and smiled. Her few remaining teeth were black, and her face thin and lined, but her blue eyes were kind. She did not speak, but returned to her cooking. He thought she must be a servant. He sat on the settle, swinging his legs nervously and watching her. Waiting for he knew not what.

And then the broken door swung open. And the open doorway darkened.

And he was there, standing against the light, in his big boots and old broad-brimmed hat, a lanky scarecrow giant.

"Th'army's past," he said, in what sounded like a broad Dorset accent. "We'll have peace now. For a bit." He sat down on the settle heavily, as if he was very tired. His sword, hung from his opposite shoulder by a broad leather strap, thumped on the wood.

Tobias studied him, out of the corner of his eye. He *was* the old man on a horse. Same popping-out eyes, though now they were green in colour. Same jutting beard and drooping moustache. He was very brown, as if he spent all his time outdoors. His face was wrinkled, especially under the eyes. It gave him a wise, patient, bloodhound look.

The servant rushed forward to pull off his boots. Underneath he wore lumps of shapeless grey socks, very coarse wool, with holes in both, from which yellow toes with black broken nails protruded. The smell in the kitchen didn't get any better.

The woman brought him a pewter pot of beer. He drank noisily until the pewter pot was tilted towards the ceiling, his Adam's apple working up and down. Then he wiped his moustache with the back of his hand and said, "You did come at an ill time, little master. But at least you do be safe now, and have enough to eat. And the little missus shall bake bread."

He smiled. God, how awful their teeth were! But a least you could understand what they said.

Tobias said, timidly, "When shall we go back, sir?"

"Go back? When thy father and mother do come

for thee. I do not know when that will be. Till then, thee do be safer with us, in spite of th'Army. Now . . ." He pulled on his boots again and rose to his feet. He was a fidgety man. You could tell he wasn't much of a one for sitting down. Or perhaps he was worried. "Now, since you must be here, I shall show you this Army and all its works, if you wish. And then you can tell those in your own time why we fought. Come!"

Tobias hesitated. He was reluctant to go out again into this strange world of dead men lying as if asleep on the grass. He was terrified of leaving the door through which he could run back into the twentieth century and the rain and the endless waiting and the Curry's vans. But young hippies are used to judging people quickly, and acting on their judgement. And he somehow trusted this old man. And it would be a shame to miss this chance to see things, as they once had been.

They went out together, the old man's hand resting quite naturally on Tobias' shoulder. That was one of Tobias' lasting memories of that time – the way people put their hands on your shoulder. It made you feel safer.

Outside stood a horse that seemed truly huge, but not very well looked after. Its coat was extremely long and shabby. Its legs were plastered with mud, up to the belly. The old man mounted with a tired grunt, and offered Tobias a large hand. Tobias scrambled up behind as best as he could, making the horse shy, and the old man say, "Steady, Tamsin, old mare!"

Then they were off, Tobias clinging to the old man's long leather coat for dear life, able to see nothing of where they were going for the old man's wide shoulders. Tobias had often ridden ponies, even bareback. But nothing as huge and broad as this. He expected to be bounced off at any moment.

The old man seemed quite clear where he was going. Every so often they would come across little groups of men, dressed in floppy hats and breeches and square-toed shoes. Carrying weapons of every sort, from long wicked-looking pistols to rusty hedging tools. They all looked dirty, weary and had stubble on their cheeks. Always, the old man's message was the same. The Army was gone. Bury the dead. Go home and sleep, but watch for the beacon fires.

They all seemed glad to be going home.

At last Tobias plucked up courage to ask, "Why are you sending them home? Aren't you going to fight?"

"They did fight, and fought well. Now they have cows to milk, and the hay to gather, before the rain ruins it. The Army is far away now." He nodded to where a patch of sunlight, in a far distant valley, revealed the crawling snake. "The Army are becoming Devon's bane, now."

"But you haven't beaten them!"

"We did begin to beat them. Oh, they look very fine and fierce at present. But they have ten thousand bellies to fill. And we have kept their bellies empty for three nights now. The only sheep and cows they found were dead and rotting down the village wells. So they are thirsty too.

"The Earl of Essex – Wait-a-bit-Bob we call him, for he's none too keen to rush into a fight – is not looking for battle this morning. He is looking for vittles. Bellies rumble, the men grumble. They haven't been paid for months. They have to live on what they can steal. They have stole precious little off us.

54

"They will be seeing visions soon. Not their holy visions, but visions of a hot pasty." The old man *spat* the words out.

They bounced on. "See the beacon fires," said the old man, pointing to the columns of smoke rising from the distant hills around the Army. "We light them to warn the people. Wherever the Army goes, the beacon fires light ahead of them. The people flee to the hills with all their animals, till the Army is past."

"Doesn't the Army chase them?"

"They send out little bands of men with carts – foragers. Then we lie behind the hedges and kill them, and give the cattle back to the people."

Tobias remembered the dead men, and the dead horse in the cart, and shuddered.

"You really hate them."

"We hate what they do. Every day, that Army eats the cows from fifty farms. Their horses eat the winter hay, so that even the cows that are left will die. Everywhere that Army goes, children will starve this winter.

"We do not wish the men dead. Half of them do not wish to be here – they want to go home and get their own hay in. Many desert every day, if they can escape the officers. Then they will steal all their way home. All we want is that they go home."

"You're not really fighting for the King, then?"

"Not outside this county of Dorset. The King is the King. It was better when he enjoyed his own, in peace. We never thought of him, except when he asked for Ship Money. We grumbled, but we paid.

"But these London merchants, who sit fat in their city, and send their poor apprentices to fight . . . nobody starves among the fat merchants of London.

They pray on their fat knees to the God that made them fat. I will show you what these merchants do! These *saints*, these whited Lambs of God!"

He spurred away towards where a church stood, on top of a low hill.

Craning his neck, Tobias could see something was very wrong with the church.

It had no windows. It stared out on the countryside like an eyeless skull.

The path from the church gate, through the low squat tombstones leaning in the long grass, was thick with horse manure, muffling the sound of Tamsin's hooves.

They went inside. No seats, only a stone bench round the wall. Tobias could tell there had never been any seats. But the awful thing was the horse manure, lying in great heaps. The stink was awful; human filth mixed up with that of horses. Urine, like the worst kind of public lavatory. Clouds of flies rose buzzing in the gathering heat. And lying, mixed in with the horse manure, masses of beautifully coloured glass, blue, green, red, yellow.

Tobias picked up one long piece; it was the most beautiful blue he had ever seen, with folds of drapery painted on it in black.

"That was once the robe of our Virgin," said the old man. "The Virgin with the Chirst-child in her arms. I have prayed to her since I was younger than you. Every day." He sounded . . . more than sad.

Tobias stared round appalled. It was *horrible* – worse than when the Fuzz smashed in Dylan's windows.

"Did the Army do *that*? But *why*?"

"The Parliament men know but one way to pray. On their feet, instead of on their knees. They stand

56

and rant at their Maker for hours at a time. It must weary God as it wearies men. They do it anywhere – in an open field or a limewashed barn. So they called our church a Popish temple, and broke it. After they had used it. It is always the same – sentries up the tower, men sleeping in the sanctuary, horses stabled in the nave. They say that in London, now, harlots ply their trade in St Paul's.

"They did not break these windows while they camped here, and the windows kept out the wind and the rain. They broke them when they left. Calling them heathen idols. They even stole shotguns from the village, and fired at the angels, because they could not reach them." He pointed up at the roof of the church.

Tobias gazed upwards at dark rafters that were covered with great carved golden-winged figures. Some had a wing missing. There was a shattered golden wing lying at his feet.

The old man picked it up with a sigh, then threw it down again on a manure heap in a gesture of despair. "The people are too poor to buy new glass. The people will not come here any more. This place of God will be a ruin."

"But why? Why can't they leave you alone, to live as you want?"

"That is a thing that has always puzzled me," said the old man. "I find it hard enough to rule my own life. And those of my good servants. How these Parliament men can be so sure they know what is best for so many . . . Their God tells them strange things. That ill-health and poverty are punishments for sin. So they drive away the poor and sick who come begging at their doors. Or hang them for witches. It is cheaper than giving them bread. They are the worst of men. I would rather have an honest thief, who does not call upon God to bless his evil-doing. Perhaps we shall have to kill them all, to get the sound of their ranting out of our ears . . ."

The old man seemed as if he would hang around the church for ever, picking up bits of wreckage, then tossing them down again. Because he wanted to mend them all, and couldn't. Tobias could only watch helplessly.

Then the church door banged open, making Tobias jump. A panting man ran up the aisle, shouting was John Oldman here, for his horse was tethered outside? The old man roused himself, and ran to him. They shouted at each other a lot, in hurried garbled voices. Tobias could only catch the odd phrase.

Three parties of cropheads. Fortifying Rempton church. . . and Master Fulwood's great house next door. Nigh a hundred men . . . with many cattle.

"Come boy." The old man ran for his horse, as if the years had dropped off him. Tobias had scarcely time to jump up behind, before they were off at a terrifying gallop.

The scene at Rempton told all. A black flag and helmeted heads on top of the tower. Long gun barrels pointing through the battlements. Black holes broken in the bottoms of the church windows, through which more guns pointed. Broken windows and pointing guns in the great house too. The house was of thick grey stone like the church, and only a few yards away. In the big walled garden that separated the two, carts were parked, their tops just showing. Horses' heads poked up above the wall with nervous pricked ears. And there was the wretched lowing complaining of many cows. Hundreds of country people had gathered in the shelter of the cottage walls.

"They will destroy the church!"

"They will kill the cattle!"

Many in the crowd carried weapons, but they were like sheep without a shepherd. Only one group of young men seemed organized. They stood in a huddle beside some very fine horses. But the horses were smeared with mud, and there was dried foam round their mouths and on the sides of their necks. Each saddle had two long holsters, from which the butts of pistols stuck out, and each young man had a short rifle hung round his neck, as well as his sword.

The young men's clothing was fine – velvet and lace, though ragged and muddy too. They did not look as if they had washed for weeks. They looked little more than schoolboys. The dark smudges of moustache and beard on their faces seemed unlikely ever to grow into anything. They had the dark wild look of motorbikers. And they were arguing with each other violently.

When John Oldman strode up, they stopped quarrelling and turned to him, like boys to a schoolmaster. They demanded to attack immediately.

"You are too fine young men to die," said John Oldman. "This place is strongly held. They know what they are doing."

As if to prove his point, there was the sound of fireworks from the church tower. Puffs of grey smoke, a whizzing in the air, and chips of stone flew off the top of the churchyard wall in all directions. Everyone ducked, even the young men. When one young man stood up again, he had a trickle of blood down his downy, ruddy cheek. He pulled out a handkerchief that was lace-edged, but grey with dirt,

59

and dabbed at his cheek over and over. Making a plague of bloodspots spread across the hanky.

John Oldman took off his hat, and raised his head slowly to a gap in the top of the wall. He studied the church and house for a long time. Then he ducked down again and said, "About sixty men and forty guns. They can hold the church for weeks, with what food they have plundered. Shall I parley with them? They must know their friends march further away all the time. If they agree to give up their plunder, and leave the church undamaged further, and agree to do no more harm till they reach Devon . . ."

The young men grumbled, but at last gave in.

John Oldman borrowed a pitchfork from a villager, and tied on the end a village woman's apron. He waved it violently above the wall. After a while, another piece of white cloth was waved from the church tower. John Oldman climbed over the wall, with a leg-up from two of the young men. Stalked away through the tombstones. There was a lot of shouting, to and from the tower. Tobias couldn't understand a word. Finally, John Oldman came back and dropped wearily over the wall.

"They will not parley. Too afraid. That if they ride out, we shall be waiting for them behind the field walls."

"Then we must have them out of there," said one of the young men. "For our Sovereign Lord the King comes this way presently. He hath been at Bristol, and comes to rejoin his army. We are sent to clear his way. I would not have him see that colour flying over yonder church, or have to creep round this village like a thief in the night, for fear of their guns!"

John Oldman sighed. "Is your life so little precious to you, Sir Ralph?" Then he sighed again, and said,

"We must wait till dark. I know a door into the cellars of that house, that they will not know of. And it is a Popish house – there is a tunnel from it to the church, for the priest. We will take the house first, when they are weary. They have enough men to hold the church. But not enough to hold the house properly."

Chapter Seven

By the time night fell, Tobias was very weary and hungry; he just wished he could go back to the farm and have supper and sleep. But when the young men began scrambling over the wall into the dark churchyard, his interest revived.

"What are they doing?"

"A ruse," said John Oldman. "You could call it a forlorn hope."

The young men wriggled away between the tombstones, a pistol in each hand. A long time seemed to pass, and then there was a flash from among the tombstones and a crash of breaking glass from the house.

Immediately, there was a rattle and flash of guns from the house; Tobias could hear something hammering on the tombstones; one or two bullets, bouncing off the stones, whizzed overhead.

Then there was only darkness and silence, and men in the house calling to those in the church. Somebody called back from the church, "Save your powder!"

Then another flash from the churchyard, and another volley from the house. And another order from the church to save powder.

It seemed to go on for a long time. Tobias kept on dozing off, only to be awakened by the next volley. Then somebody came up to John Oldman.

"We have broke in the cellar window, but it is too small to climb through." He glanced at Tobias. "This boy could wriggle through."

John Oldman thought a long time, then he raised his head.

"Will you do it for us, boy? Go through the window and unbar the cellar door? It will save lives . . ."

Tobias took a deep breath, then nodded. Dad would have wanted him to save lives, and it didn't sound *too* dangerous.

"Go with William then," said the old man.

They seemed to creep a long way in the dark; Tobias placed his feet carefully to avoid making any noise. And then the bulk of the house was looming over them. There didn't seem any defenders this side; there were no windows except one tiny one, and the heavy low door close to it. Now Tobias understood what was going on in the churchyard on the other side of the house. It was a diversion. There came another burst of firing from the tombstones.

"Now!" said the man, and thrust Tobias bodily through the window with big hands round his waist. Tobias could have screeched as something raked the skin on his ribs under his shirt. Not all the broken glass had been removed. He fell inside on his hands, and nearly did a somersault as his legs were bundled through after him.

He peered around. It was a pitchy dark, except for

the dim square of the window, with the man's head. "Go to the door," said the man, and vanished as the firing stopped outside the house. Tobias was on his own.

He started to creep to where he knew the door should be. And immediately bumped into something. He felt it – rough wood, curving. It must be a great big barrel. He tried to work round it, and hit another barrel. There was a whole row of them; there was no way through. He kept on creeping and groping, and then he fell over something else. The cellar was packed with old junk. He picked himself up.

Even the pale square of the window had vanished; he was in total blackness. He called softly to the man; the man didn't answer. Outside the house, there was another outbreak of firing.

He felt like weeping. It had seemed so easy, from the outside. The window hadn't seemed five feet from the door. But now, he groped his way through a hopeless maze, from blackness to blackness, falling over again and again. Cobwebs brushed his face, clung to his mouth. He thought he would go mad. It couldn't get any worse than this.

And then, above, a door opened. From inside the house. A faint glimmer of light. A candle, outlining a stone flight of stairs. And a pair of legs in big boots coming shuffling down.

He wriggled himself deep into a shadow behind a barrel, not daring to breathe. They had heard his fall, the men above. They had come for him. They would shoot him. The legs passed within a yard of him. Then they stopped, seeming to listen. Tobias was sure the man would hear his panting. The legs gave a bad-tempered mutter, "Ah, there you are!"

Tobias nearly ran out from the shadow, with his hands in the air, before the shot came.

Just in time, he heard the chink of glass. Saw a hand reaching down two feet from his nose . . .

For a dark bottle. And a second dark bottle. And a third. The man sighed with satisfaction; the feet turned round and made their way back towards the stairs.

Tobias could not believe his own happiness when the door above closed, dropping him into sooty velvet darkness again. But not hopeless dark now. In the candlelight, he had seen the stairs, the wall, the clear space.

At the far end of the clear space, which he walked along with one hand against the wall and one in front of him, was the door. He felt for the bar that must hold it shut. Felt it move a fraction and put his shoulder to it.

The door swung open a crack, letting the blessed blue of night in, and the smell of green things to blow away the cobwebs clinging to his face.

Another burst of firing on the far side of the house. A hand flung the door open, grabbed Tobias by the shirt and pulled him out of the way, and many men bundled past him. Tobias saw the glimmer of a lantern, and the glint of its light on the long barrels of pistols. Then he was alone again. He felt his way back slowly and quietly to John Oldman. It seemed to take for ever.

"Well done, boy!" Oldman's big hand was firm and strong on his shoulder, giving comfort, quietening his frantic panting. "Now watch!"

The big house was all silent again. Then came fresh banging and flashing. From the churchyard. From the house windows.

And then flashing and banging inside the house itself. Wild unnerving cries. A horrible scream that seemed to go on and on. Then another silence broken only by a wailing sobbing.

"Good," said John Oldman. "They caught them with their dragons discharged. There is the signal. The house is ours. I must go and trace that priest tunnel for them. Stay here. Your work is done."

Tobias was glad to. Particularly as John Oldman had pressed some kind of thick coarse rug or blanket round him. He snuggled down, still shivering, and fell asleep.

Much later, he was startled awake by a fresh burst of firing. He staggered upright, and peered over the wall.

This time the flashing came from inside the high windows of the church.

Then the flashing only came from the thin windowslits in the church tower.

Then a smell of woodsmoke reached his nostrils, mingling with the autumn Guy Fawkes smell of gunpowder. Billows of grey smoke belched from every windowslit of the tower, drifting through the churchyard trees like ghosts in the moonlight. The men on top of the tower were cursing and coughing, and still firing their guns in all directions, with red flashes that lit up the drifting smoke like a scene out of hell.

He wondered who had set the church on fire. He thought he ought to go and see.

But his legs were *so* weary. And it was so warm inside the blanket, that smelt of horses. And he had done his work; John Oldman said his work was done. John Oldman said to stay and rest . . .

He lay down and slept again.

The next part might almost have been a dream. He seemed to be awakened by shouting, the running of many feet.

Someone shouting, "The King comes!"

It was still dark. But there were torches held by unsteady hands, that flickered and flared and dripped, giving a weak uncertain red light.

Tobias didn't get up. He told himself he was too tired, too warm inside the rough blanket. But really, he was too scared. He stayed in a huddle at the foot of the wall, staring through a forest of legs.

Then there was a murmur, and everyone was kneeling down. And Tobias saw the King. Sitting on the back of a great black horse. How little he looked; not much bigger than Tobias himself. He wore a black breastplate, but no helmet. His hair was long and dark, in ringlets, and looked very greasy. Draped over his shoulders, and covering the rump of the horse, was a long dark cloak of something soft like velvet, with a big star in one corner.

How high his forehead was! How tiny yet how long his pointed beard.

His eyes flickered here, there and everywhere.

There he sat.

The horse was restless, and the King's little hand kept reining it in. Or did the restlessness come from the King's hand, making the horse nervous?

Many hands reached up from the kneeling figures, to touch the King's booted legs. The King allowed it, but he did not like it. His little mouth tightened.

John Oldman was talking to the King now. The only one not kneeling, apart from the King's own officers. John Oldman pointed to Tobias, lying huddled at the foot of the wall. The King's eyes rested for a moment on Tobias. They were dark and very sad.

Then the King suddenly smiled; his whole face lit up. He said something to John Oldman and put some tiny thing in his hand. Then he hauled on the reins and spurred away, as if he had more urgent business elsewhere; and was gone into the night.

The people wandered off. Tobias slept again.

Chapter Eight

He woke up in the cool brightness of early morning.
The sun, just coming above the trees, threw Tobias'
blue shadow on the churchyard wall. There was dew
on the grass, soaking it silver-white, making it look
precious. Birds were singing. The sky was a pale, pale
blue, and cloudless from horizon to horizon. All the
night before seemed like a dream, a bad dream. The
morning was washing him clean of it.

Over the churchyard wall, Tobias heard voices.
Cheerful slow gossiping country voices, with no fear
in them. The sound of spades digging, thudding into
the ground, clinking on stones. The sweet smell of
soil.

Tobias felt suddenly terribly hungry. He wondered
if the voices over the wall had anything to eat. Still
clutching the blanket round him, against the morning
chill, he peered over the wall.

He saw a very large hole with straight-cut sides and
two men down it, backs bent. A big mound of

crumbly red earth with pale worms wriggling in it, dropping and coiling. And besides the earth . . .

Three men lay naked. The yellow soles of their feet and their big knobbly toes were towards Tobias. So he couldn't see their faces properly. But their mouths were open, showing what was left of their teeth, and their noses were pointing to the pale blue sky.

So still. So pale. A churchyard starling flew down and perched on the big toe of the fat one in the middle.

It was only then that Tobias believed they were dead.

He didn't feel frightened. He just felt incredibly *weird*. He just couldn't stop staring.

The starling on the man's toe chirruped cheerfully.

A large hand fell on Tobias' shoulder. He looked round with a great start. But it was only John Oldman, smiling at him sadly.

"Did you sleep well, little master?"

"Why are they burying them without any clothes on?"

John Oldman shrugged. "Who could afford to buy them a shroud? The people here are poor."

"But they must have *had* clothes!"

"We need their shirts and britches, as we need their pistols."

"What – with all *blood* on them?"

"Blood and worse than blood. The wives will wash them as clean as they can. They will keep some poor King's man warm. Better a bloody shirt in a blizzard than naked."

"But . . . they're *people*!"

"The priest will read a service over them; though not one to their liking. And, to please you, I will put a

70

posie on their grave, to mark the anniversary of their death."

"I feel sick."

"Time you broke your fast. Come into the house and I will find you something. If they've left anything."

"If I hadn't opened that door, they'd still be alive."

"If you hadn't opened that door, some village lad would have been fetched to open it. If that door hadn't been opened, we might be burying twenty. This is a light loss. We took them by surprise and they threw down their arms. Saving those in the church tower, and we lit a little fire on the stair to smoke them out. They came down, after half an hour's kippering. And the people have their cows back. And the King has enough arms for a new troop of horse."

"What will you do . . . to the others?"

"Well, we couldn't spare the powder to shoot 'em, and we hadn't the vittles to feed 'em. So we took their oath to fight against the King no more, and sent them home to gather their harvest. All bar the officers, and they're all dead but two. The King's men took them to Dorchester gaol."

"The King . . ." said Tobias dreamily.

"Come and eat your bread, before somebody else does."

They rode home through quiet fields. The people were gathering in the corn. The men in long-sleeved loose shirts, swinging their scythes in a great line. The women behind, faceless inside their bonnets, bending and gathering and tying in bundles and stacking in stooks. And the children, even the little children who could hardly toddle, searching among

71

the stubble for loose heads of corn and putting them in baskets.

"There will be enough for everyone," said John Oldman, "I think."

"Suppose the Army comes back?" The fear of the Army was in Tobias now, like the fear of the Fuzz.

"I do not think that Army will come back," said John Oldman thoughtfully. "I think that Army is lost. Wait-a-bit-Bob does not know what he wants to do. Oh, he will relieve Lyme, no doubt. Capture a few towns, then march out again. And the people will be loyal to the King, as before.

"But there is no other army in the west for him to fight. The King will block their way home, and let them wander till their legs founder. There is something about the far west that mazes the mind and breeds dreams. Already, my Lord of Essex is caught in that dream, though he does not know it. No, that Army will not return."

"Was the King pleased?" asked Tobias timidly.

"As pleased as he ever is. He is lost in a dream much worse than Wait-a-bit-Bob's. Wait-a-bit-Bob will come home to his wife and children again. I think this King will die, and he knows it."

"Oh," said Tobias, very impressed. He wondered whether he ought to say anything of what he knew from history lessons, but decided not to. That would be cheating in some way.

"The King was amused to hear of you getting lost in that cellar in the dark, not knowing which way to turn. He said now you would know how it felt to be a King."

"Oh," said Tobias again. That was a witty thing to say, he thought but very sad.

"The King sent you his portrait. He is generous to

those who serve him, in little things. He likes to give gifts."

John Oldman passed something back over his shoulder. Something that glinted tiny and round between his massive finger and thumb. Tobias extracted it with great care. It was a gold coin, with the King's head on one side. Tobias put it gingerly in the only pocket of his jeans that had no hole in it.

John Oldman reined in the horse on the hill above the farm. The hill from which Tobias had first seen the Army. All around, in the sunset, the hump-backed hills glowed peaceful and green. There were very white sheep, with black faces, grazing in small flocks, all over the hillsides, far and near.

"This is my place," said John Oldman. "Armies come and armies go, but this is my place."

Somehow, Tobias knew that things were coming to an end. Some kind of time was running out.

"Will you still help us?" he asked desperately, staring at the broad leather-clad shoulders in front of him. Nothing had got any better; Mum was still missing, Dad in prison, the bus smashed and home so far away. He felt like crying.

"You came to my time, little master," said John Oldman gently. "It was a bad time, but we kept you safe. I cannot come to your time. In your time, I am a few old bones in a churchyard. As *you* will be, when your course is run."

A cold evening breeze crept up behind Tobias, so that he shivered.

"My father is in prison."

"What is your father?"

"He makes pots and jugs."

"That is an honest trade. Why is he in prison? Is he a Catholic?"

"No – he's a Quaker."

John Oldman laughed ruefully. "Times do not change much. He is a Quaker, and he is in prison. There are many Quakers in prison in *my* time. For their beliefs. They are fearsome men, Quakers. Fearsome in their hatred of war and love of peace. I do not think any great harm will come to your father. The soul of a Quaker is in the hand of God."

"My mother is lost . . ."

"What is lost may yet be found . . ."

"The Fuzz smashed our bus. Like the Army smashed your church!"

"Would you have me and my lads charge them down, firing our pistols?"

For a moment, Tobias had that glorious vision. He wanted to shout "Yes, yes!"

"Would your father think that a good thing, Tobias?"

"No," Tobias said reluctantly.

"Well then! I think you will find an old man will yet come charging to your aid, Tobias. We old men can be very fierce, when those we love are threatened."

"What do you mean? *What* old man?"

John Oldman shook his head. "Let us go and find your sister, and the bread she has been baking."

"God, it's so *cold*," said Tobias. "I wish I could sleep."

"Like a bit more bread?" asked Greta. "There's one little loaf left."

"Better than nothing," said Tobias ungraciously. "It's a good chew. Gives you something to do."

He felt her hand nudge him, in the cold silent dark

74

of the barn, and took the lump of bread off her. It was as tough as an old boot, but it tasted nice, even without any butter on it. He chewed and stared moodily at the dim slits of dark blue that were the windows in the barn wall. It seemed *years* since John Oldman had said goodbye, and barred the door of the kitchen against them, with terrible finality. Saying that they must accept what was going to happen to them; that he could interfere with time no more. It seemed so stupid, lying here in their damp sleeping bags on the straw, when there was a blazing fire and a good feather-bed next door.

Was the blue of the slits in the wall getting a bit lighter?

"Someone's tooting," said Greta. "Out on the road."

"Who'd be out there, this time of night?" said Tobias crossly.

But there *was* somebody tooting. And when Tobias got out of his sleeping bag and went to the barn door, there were the lights of a vehicle shining in the road beyond the field.

The tooting came again. Oddly, Tobias thought it was like the way that Dad tooted. It sounded like Dylan the bus.

Don't be ridiculous! Dozens of buses had the same kind of horn. Vans too. And dozens of people hooted their horns like Dad. There were only about six ways of tooting a horn.

Could be anybody. In fact, somebody tooting a horn in this lonely place in the middle of the night might be mad . . . dangerous. The truth was that Dad was in the nick, Dylan smashed to bits, and that was the end of it. It was silly to expect John Oldman to work *miracles*.

Whoever it was in the road drove off. Immediately, Tobias wished he *had* gone and seen who it was. Why had he got so suspicious of everybody, all of a sudden?

And why was he, like a silly baby, crawling around in the straw looking for the statue of the old man on a horse, so he could plead with it again to make things better?

He searched and searched for the statue, with increasing panic. It wasn't there. It wasn't anywhere. It was gone.

He went back to Greta, unable to speak because he felt he might cry again. Then he grunted, "Any more bread?"

"I ate the last," said Greta. "It's all gone."

The statue was gone, the bread was gone. There was no proof any more that John Oldman had ever existed, that he wasn't just a hunger-dream. The only reality was the dark, and the cold, and the rain still falling outside.

Until, as he wriggled back into the bag, something nipped him in the belly, and he groped around to find out what it was.

The tiny gold coin; the portrait of the King. He didn't dare take it out for fear of losing it in the dark. But he knew it was there.

And so he slept.

Chapter Nine

"They're here!" called a loud voice. "Safe and sound. Fast asleep, the little monkeys."

The voice sounded very bossy, and a bit cross, but awfully glad underneath.

Grandpa's voice. But Grandpa was away on a dig in . . .

Tobias opened his eyes. It *was* Grandpa; his bald head with the strand of hair plastered across the front of it. Grandpa all shining in a shaft of sunlight. And here was Grandma coming in, in her jeans and anorak. And then Dad, not in the nick after all.

Tobias staggered to his feet, trying to rub the sleep out of his eyes. The barn door was wide open.

And there, across the fields, was Dylan. With all its windows intact, shining in the sun.

"Where's Mum?"

"In hospital," said Dad. "But she's going to be all right."

"So John Oldman can work miracles after all!"

"Who's this John Oldman?" asked Grandpa sharply.

Tobias found it impossible to explain. So he just gestured wildly at the doorway that led into the kitchen.

Only there was no door there any more. Only a place where a door had once been. All bricked up and a long time ago. Cobwebs growing across the bricks. Old, old bricks.

It was unbearable. Tobias ran round the outside of the barn. With Grandpa in hot pursuit.

They both stood and stared at what they found.

The ragged edge of broken stonework, where the barn ended. Low mounds under grass.

Grandpa's archaeologist's eye read it like a book. "There must have been a big farmhouse here once," he said. "You can still see the foundations. Look, the doorway to the outside was here – doorstep's still in place, under the turf. And I'm sure this was a big fireplace, big enough to roast a whole ox in."

At least the hilltop was still there. And the little flocks of sheep. Different sort of sheep, that was all. Fatter, with white faces.

Then Tobias knew that John Oldman was gone for ever. Just a few old bones in the churchyard . . .

Tobias' eyes filled with tears. "Goodbye," he whispered. "And thanks."

Chapter Ten

Tobias took his father for a walk, after they left the hospital.

"Are you sure Mum's going to be all right?"

"The specialist thinks so. They can't find any lasting damage. Her brain-scan was normal, and there's no bones broken. But they'll keep her in a few more days, because she's been in a coma. They want to make sure, before they let her go home. Didn't she seem all right to you?"

"What happened to her?"

"She was walking to Walchester in the cold and rain, and she fell in front of a passing car. They think she must've fainted or something. So she was rushed into hospital, and she was unconscious for three days, and couldn't tell anybody about *you*."

"How did Grandpa get here?"

"The police found Mum's driving licence in her bag, and went to our house at home. The house was locked up, but Aunty Liz was seeing to the goats. She told them Grandpa was in Cyprus and they traced him through the university. He flew straight home. And he sort of went berserk. His daughter at death's door, two kids vanished off the face of the earth, smashed-up bus and his Quaker pacifist son-in-law in the nick charged with attempted murder. He went and had a blazing row with the Chief Constable. Then he rang up Sir David Plumbley, the famous left-wing solicitor – he's an old mate of Grandpa's and the police are absolutely terrified of him.

"Then Grandpa got on to the telly people, who are also old mates of his, from the time he did that series "Old Stone, Old Bone". They got him the film taken from the helicopter, of the police smashing up Dylan. *And* they were dead keen to do a programme on police brutality. And then Grandpa began ringing up Labour MPs he knew . . . even the shadow Home Secretary! I think he was going to start World War III. One very powerful angry old man, charging to the rescue!

"The police just went to pieces. They dropped the charges against me. They had the bus repaired at their own expense. And they've been looking for you, night and day, ever since. They really have scoured the county. I can't think of how they came to miss your barn."

"Perhaps we weren't there when they came," said Tobias thoughtfully. He looked across at Grandpa, waiting for them on the steps of the hospital. Yes, he *was* like John Oldman in a way. Quick, busy, fierce. Fierce when those he loved were threatened.

John Oldman had worked no miracle. But John Oldman had been right. Another old man had come. Tobias had always been rather scared of Grandpa, but suddenly he loved him. Though how he would ever show it was another matter. Grandpa disliked a fuss, as John Oldman had disliked a fuss . . .

"But . . . supposing we hadn't *had* Grandpa? What about the other people in the hippie convoy who didn't have a Grandpa like that?"

Dad sighed. "You're starting to sound like your Mum."

"But the Fuzz are going to get away with it. Those other people have lost their buses. They'll have nowhere to live this winter . . ."

"Look, Tobias, don't be too hard on the Fuzz. They were doing what they were told. The farmers . . . most of the people watching on telly . . . they *wanted* the hippy convoy stopped. Broken up and scattered. So the Fuzz did what people wanted. Then the same people turn on them and start screaming about police brutality, trying to dump all the blame on the Fuzz for what they wanted themselves. It's always that way."

"Yeah," said Tobias. He remembered the Army. Fat London merchants who sent their apprentices to steal Dorset cows and smash Dorset churches, and starve Dorset children.

"The Fuzz are like guard-dogs," said Dad. "People take nice Alsatian pups and teach them to bite. Then the dog gets over-excited and bites the wrong person, and they take the dog away and destroy it. The Fuzz are only ordinary people inside those uniforms. They still bleed inside the uniforms. The uniforms just stop *us* seeing the bleeding, when *they're* hurt."

Tobias remembered the three dead naked men in the churchyard.

"Yeah," he said again. It suddenly all seemed too difficult.

Grandpa and Grandma were staying at a posh hotel they knew in Bridport. Dad and Greta and Tobias went to spend the night with them. Next afternoon, Grandma took Greta and Tobias shopping, while Dad and Grandpa went to see Mum in hospital.

Tobias found shopping with Grandma embarrassing. She wasn't at all like a *real* grannie. She wore khaki trousers and a bush-jacket and tied her long red hair back in a ponytail and smoked in the street and even when she was buying things, keeping her fag in her mouth and squinting up her eyes against the smoke. She was bossy, and said rude things if the shop assistants weren't quick and helpful. She wasn't very old, for a Grannie, and Tobias thought she didn't much like being one. But she was dead generous, and would buy you anything, even if you said you only *quite* liked it. Greta made the most of it, little pig. Laura Ashley night-dresses . . . Mum would go mad when she found out.

Tobias sort of drifted gently away. There was a more interesting shop next door. A big black-and-white half-timbered shop that looked really old. It had a notice screwed to the front, saying it had once been an inn, and that Charles II had slept there. It was full of tourist gifts and pottery. The pottery was quite good, but not as good as Dad's.

And then he saw it, right at the back of the shop. Perched on top of a glass case full of with-it jewellery. Battered, blackened, chipped but still quite recognizable.

The Old Man on a Horse.

He crept in; peered up at it. The bulging eyes

82

stared down at him, impassive. Time had not changed him.

"That's a very old figure!" said the lady of the shop, with a kind smile. "That used to be on the roof of this inn. It was here when Charles II stayed here. We brought it down for safe keeping, when it started to crack."

"What's it for?"

"It was to protect the house. That's all we know."

"Oh!"

"Tobias!" called Grandma from the shop-door. "There you are! Time for lunch."

"Hello," whispered Tobias. The old man still said nothing. He must have looked very fine on the rooftop, before they brought him down, astride the wild skies. As he had looked on the hilltop in real life, with his horse tired from rough riding, and the long pistols sticking from his holsters.

Protect the house. Protect the land. Protect the cattle. Protect the children. King, armies, fat merchants of London; he had outlived them all.

"Thanks," said Tobias, again, remembering and clutching the King's coin in his jeans pocket.

HAUNTINGS by Hippo Books is a new series of excellent ghost stories for older readers.

Ghost Abbey by Robert Westall
When Maggie and her family move into a run-down old abbey, they begin to notice some very strange things going on in the rambling old building. Is there any truth in the rumour that the abbey is haunted?

Don't Go Near the Water by Carolyn Sloan
Brendan knew instinctively that he shouldn't go near Blackwater Lake. Especially that summer, when the water level was so low. But what was the dark secret that lurked in the depths of the lake?

Voices by Joan Aiken
Julia had been told by people in the village that Harkin House was haunted. And ever since moving in to the house for the summer, she'd been troubled by violent dreams. What had happened in the old house's turbulent past?

The Nightmare Man by Tessa Krailing
Alex first sees the man of his darkest dreams at Stackfield Pond. And soon afterwards he and his family move in to the old house near the pond — End House — and the nightmare man becomes more than just a dream.

A Wish at the Baby's Grave by Angela Bull
Desperate for some money, Cathy makes a wish for some at the baby's grave in the local cemetery. Straight afterwards, she finds a job at an old bakery. But there's something very strange about the bakery and the two Germans who work there. . .

The Bone-Dog by Susan Price
Susan can hardly believe her eyes when her uncle Bryan makes her a pet out of an old fox-fur, a bone and some drops of blood — and then brings it to life. It's wonderful to have a pet which follows her every command — until the bone-dog starts to obey even her unconscious thoughts. . .

All on a Winter's Day by Lisa Taylor
Lucy and Hugh wake up suddenly one wintry morning to find everything's changed — their mother's disappeared, the house is different, and there are two ghostly children and their evil-looking aunt in the house. What has happened?

The Old Man on a Horse by Robert Westall
Tobias couldn't understand what was happening. His parents and little sister had gone to Stonehenge with the hippies, and his father was arrested. Then his mother disappeared. But while sheltering with his sister in a barn, he finds a statue of an old man on a horse, and Tobias and Greta find themselves transported to the time of the Civil War. . .

Look out for these forthcoming titles in the HAUNTING series:
The Rain Ghost by Garry Kilworth
The Haunting of Sophy Bartholomew by Elizabeth Lindsay

SAMANTHA SLADE

Samantha Slade's an ordinary girl living in an ordinary town; but when she starts a job out of school babysitting for the Brown children, her uneventful life is turned upside down. Because when Dr Brown tells Samantha her children are little monsters, poor Sam doesn't realize that they really *are* monsters! Lupi turns into a werewolf when the moon is full, and Drake sprouts fangs, drinks tomato ketchup by the crateful and concocts the most amazing potions in his laboratory!

Book 1: Monster-Sitter

When Samantha Slade agrees to let Lupi and Drake Brown, the two children she babysits, help her with the school Halloween party, she finds she's created the most realistic haunted house ever! Lupi turns into a real werewolf, the fake creepie crawlies become alive, and the whole thing turns into a riot of terrified kids . . .

Book 2: Confessions of a Teenage Frog

Samantha Slade should have known better than to accept help from Lupi and Drake when she's campaigning to become class president. Drake makes her a "greatness potion", and before she knows it, she's been turned into a frog! Will Drake be able to turn her back again before she has to make her big speech for the campaign?

Other titles in the SAMANTHA SLADE series:
Book 3 **Our Friend, Public Nuisance No 1**
Book 4 **The Terrors of Rock and Roll**

HIPPO BOOKS FOR OLDER READERS

If you enjoy a good read, look out for all the Hippo books that are available for older readers. You'll find gripping adventure stories, romance novels, spooky ghost stories and all sorts of fun fiction.

CHEERLEADERS NO 2:		
GETTING EVEN	Christopher Pike	£1.25
CHEERLEADERS NO 3:		
RUMOURS	Caroline B Cooney	£1.25
ANIMAL INN 1: PETS		
ARE FOR KEEPS	Virginia Vail	£1.50
MEGASTAR	Jean Ure	£1.50
SOMERSAULTS	Michael Hardcastle	£1.50
THE LITTLE		
GYMNAST	Sheila Haigh	£1.25
CREEPS	Tim Schoch	£1.50
THE GREAT FLOOD		
MYSTERY	Jane Curry	£1.75
GET LAVINIA		
GOODBODY!	Roger Collinson	£1.25
AM I GOING WITH		
YOU?	Thurley Fowler	£1.25
THE KARATE KID:		
PART II	B B Hiller	£1.25
KEVIN AND THE IRON		
POODLE	J K Hooper	£1.25

You'll find these and many more fun Hippo books at your local bookseller, or you can order them direct. Just send off to *Customer Services, Hippo Books, Westfield Road, Southam, Leamington Spa, Warwickshire CV33 OJH*, not forgetting to enclose a cheque or postal order for the price of the book(s) plus 30p per book for postage and packing.

HIPPO BESTSELLERS

If you enjoyed this book, why not look out for other
bestselling Hippo titles. You'll find gripping novels, fun
activity books, fascinating non-fiction, crazy humour
and sensational poetry books for all ages and tastes.

THE GHOSTBUSTERS STORYBOOK	Anne Digby	£2.50
SNOOKERED	Michael Hardcastle	£1.50
BENJI THE HUNTED	Walt Disney Company	£2.25
NELLIE AND THE DRAGON	Elizabeth Lindsay	£1.75
ALIENS IN THE FAMILY	Margaret Mahy	£1.50
HARRIET AND THE CROCODILES	Martin Waddell	£1.25
MAKE ME A STAR 1: PRIME TIME	Susan Beth Pfeffer	£1.50
THE SPRING BOOK	Troy Alexander	£2.25
SLEUTH!	Sherlock Ransford	£1.50
THE SPOOKTACULAR JOKE BOOK	Theodore Freek	£1.25
ROLAND RAT'S RODENT JOKE BOOK		£1.25
THE LITTLE VAMPIRE	Angela Sommer-Bodenberg	£1.25
POSTMAN PAT AND THE GREENDALE GHOST	John Cunliffe	£1.50
POSTMAN PAT AND THE CHRISTMAS PUDDING	John Cunliffe	£1.50

You'll find these and many more fun Hippo books at
your local bookseller, or you can order them direct. Just
send off to *Customer Services, Hippo Books, Westfield
Road, Southam, Leamington Spa, Warwickshire CV33
OJH*, not forgetting to enclose a cheque or postal order
for the price of the book(s) plus 30p per book for postage
and packing.

THE STEPSISTERS

When Paige's Dad marries Virginia Guthrie from Atlanta, she's thrilled that he's found someone to make him happy. But how will she get on with her new stepbrother and stepsisters? Especially Katie, the beautiful blonde fifteen-year-old, who looks like a model and can charm her way out of anything!

1   The War Between the Sisters   £1.75

Not only does Paige have to share her room with her stepsister, Katie, but then she finds that Jake, the boy she's fallen in love with, finds Katie totally irresisitible. Paige's jealousy leads her to do some pretty stupid things to get her own back . . .

2   The Sister Trap   £1.75

Paige is delighted when she gets a job working on the school magazine. Especially when she becomes friendly with the magazine editor, Ben. But her jealousies over her beautiful stepsister, Katie, flare up again when Ben starts taking a lot of interest in Katie's swimming career.

Look out for these new titles in
THE STEPSISTERS series:
3   Bad Sisters
4   Sisters in Charge

You will find these and many more great Hippo books at your local bookseller, or you can order them direct. Just send off to *Customer Services, Hippo Books, Westfield Road, Southam, Leamington Spa, Warwickshire CV33 0JH*, not forgetting to enclose a cheque or postal order for the price of the book(s) plus 30p per book for postage and packing.